She knew that she didn't really ~~owe~~ him an explan~~ation~~.

After all, he ~~...~~ d been done in the ~~...~~ had a right to kno~~w...~~ ise, so she felt the ~~...~~ she'd gone back on it.

"I know I promised that you'd have the final say, but I've got people I answer to and they insisted that the segment go on tonight as is. It turned out pretty well, I thought." She crossed her fingers that he saw it that way, too.

"You lied to me." It wasn't an accusation but a flat statement. It carried with it not anger, but a note of genuine disappointment. And that made her feel worse than if he'd launched into a tirade.

"I didn't lie," she replied. "I had every intention of showing you the clip first." When he said nothing, she felt uncomfortable, despite the fact that this ultimately wasn't really her fault. "The station manager wanted to air it before the other stations got it. I'm sorry, but these things happen. Listen, if you want me to make it up to you—" she began, not really certain where this would ultimately go.

He cut her short with two words. "I do."

MATCHMAKING MAMAS:
Playing Cupid. Arranging dates.
What are mothers for?

Dear Reader,

Sometimes it takes just one word, one passing incident to make a story start coming together for a writer. The "incident" that made this story begin to form was a chance conversation struck up in line at my local post office last Christmas season. The place was packed with impatient people who all had somewhere else to be if only they could take care of whatever business had brought them to the post office—mailing Christmas packages comes to mind.

I was as trapped as everyone else, standing in line behind this young woman. She, however, didn't have her arms filled with packages that needed to be mailed "yesterday." She was there to pick up a box that needed a signature. But her arms weren't empty. She was holding on to—or trying to hold on to—this energized ball of flying fur that seemed determined to make a break for it up or down the young woman's arms.

Since I will, given half a chance, strike up a conversation with a box of oatmeal cookies to make the time go faster, I made a comment that the dog—a puppy really—looked about as anxious to leave as I was. The woman laughed, saying that the puppy, which she'd picked up at our local shelter (which takes in all manners of stray animals—even the occasional chicken and turtle—and puts nothing to death, not even ill-tempered opossums), was like this *all* the time. I sympathized, saying it was very cute and then asked its name, thinking that would be my clue to its gender. I didn't want to come right out and ask if it was a male or female. Some owners are funny about their pets when it comes to that.

The puppy's name, it turned out, was Pancakes. It didn't clue me in as to whether the puppy was a male or female, but suddenly a kernel of an idea came to me, and by the time I was able to leave the post office, Christmas package free, I had the makings of another story in my head. Just goes to prove that the post office works in mysterious ways.

As always, I would like to thank you for taking the time to read my book—I will never take you for granted—and from the bottom of my heart, I wish you someone to love who loves you back.

All the best,

Marie

Twice a Hero, Always Her Man

—

Marie Ferrarella

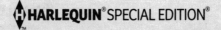

HARLEQUIN® SPECIAL EDITION®

Recycling programs
for this product may
not exist in your area.

ISBN-13: 978-0-373-62321-1

Twice a Hero, Always Her Man

Printed in U.S.A.

www.Harlequin.com

USA TODAY bestselling and RITA® Award—winning author **Marie Ferrarella** has written more than two hundred and fifty books for Harlequin, some under the name Marie Nicole. Her romances are beloved by fans worldwide. Visit her website, marieferrarella.com.

To Charlie
For stepping up
And
Taking care of me
When I couldn't.
After all these years,
You still manage to surprise me.

Prologue

"Oh, Maizie, it's just breaking my heart, seeing her like this."

Maizie Sommers quietly pushed the gaily decorated box of triple-ply tissues she kept on her desk toward her friend, waiting for the woman to collect herself. Connie Williams had called her first thing this morning, asking to see her.

Maizie knew from her friend's tone of voice that she wasn't asking to see her in her professional capacity— at least not in her professional capacity as an award-winning Realtor.

But Maizie had another vocation, an altruistic one that was near and dear to her heart, as it was to the hearts of her two dearest, lifelong friends, Theresa Manetti and Cecilia Parnell. All three were career women who did quite well in their respective chosen fields. But it was the one avocation that they had in common that brought them the most joy. The one that carried no monetary reward whatsoever, just one that made them feel good.

All three were matchmakers.

It had begun quite innocently enough. The three of them had been friends since the third grade. In the years that followed, they had gone through all the milestones of life together, great and small—not the least of which was widowhood. And all three were also blessed with children. Maizie had a daughter, as did Cecilia, while Theresa had a daughter *and* a son.

Their four children were all successful in their own rights—and they were also maddeningly single. Until Maizie decided that her daughter, an ob-gyn, needed more in her life than just delivering other people's babies. She needed a private life of her own. Joining forces with her two friends, Maizie began to closely monitor and review the wide variety of people all three of them dealt with.

Thanks to their professions—Theresa ran a catering company, while Cecilia had a thriving housecleaning service—Maizie quickly and secretly found the perfect "someone" for her daughter.

Theresa and Cecilia were quick to follow her example, and soon all three of *their* children were matched to their soul mates, as well.

Nothing bred more success than initial success and so a passion was born. Maizie, Theresa and Cecilia began helping the children of other friends, all while always managing to keep the principals involved in the dark, thinking it was fate rather than three very artful women that had intervened in their lives for the better.

So it didn't surprise Maizie at all to be sitting in her office today across from one of her friends, quietly waiting for the request she knew was coming. Connie wanted her to find someone for her daughter, a reporter with a prominent local news station.

Connie pulled out a tissue and wiped away the tears that had slid down her cheek despite her best efforts to the contrary.

"Ellie puts up a brave front and whenever I ask her, she tells me that she's fine, but she's *not* fine. A mother knows, Maizie," the older woman insisted, stifling a sob.

Maizie offered her an understanding smile. "Truer words were never spoken," she agreed. Then, gently, Maizie asked her friend, "How long has it been now?"

"Two years," Connie answered. She didn't even have to pause to think. She knew it to the exact day. Remembered how stricken her daughter had been when she'd found out that her husband, a recently discharged, highly decorated Marine sergeant had been killed while trying to save a couple who were being robbed at a convenience store.

"She goes on with her life, goes on with her career, but I know in my heart nothing's changed. If anything, she works harder these days, spends long hours both in the field on assignment and at the studio, overseeing the editing of her work, but it's like everything froze inside her since that day."

Maizie nodded. "I can imagine how awful it must have been for Ellie to find out that the news story she was being sent to cover involved her own husband."

There had been a mix-up when the story had come over the wire and the name of the hero of the piece had been accidentally switched for the name of the owner of the convenience store where the robbery had occurred. When Ellie and her cameraman had arrived on the scene, the ambulance had already come and gone. It wasn't until she was in the middle of covering the story, talking to the two grateful people her husband had saved, that her cell phone had rung. Someone from the hospital was calling her to notify Ellie that her husband had been shot and had died en route.

"Ellie went numb when the call on her cell came in. The poor thing barely kept from fainting in front of everyone. Her studio was exceedingly sympathetic, and Ellie, well, she just froze up inside that awful, awful night and she still hasn't come around, no matter what she tries to tell me to the contrary."

Connie looked at the woman she was counting on to change things for her daughter, her eyes eloquently entreating her for help.

"Maizie, she's only thirty years old. Thirty is much too young to resign from life the way she has. Ellie has so much to offer. It's just killing me to see her like this." Connie pressed her lips together. "If I say anything to her, she just smiles and tells me not to worry. How can I not worry?" she asked.

Maizie placed her hand over her friend's in a comforting gesture, one mother reaching out to another. "I'm glad you came, Connie. Leave this to me."

The woman hesitated, her gratitude warring with a host of other feelings—and one main one that she gave voice to now. "If Ellie knew I was trying to find someone for her—"

"*You're* not," Maizie pointed out. "Let me look into this and I'll get back to you," she promised. In her mind, she was already summoning her friends for an evening card game, happily telling them that they had a brand-new assignment of the heart.

Nothing was more satisfying to them—except, of course, for the successful execution of said operation.

Maizie couldn't wait.

Chapter One

It felt as if mornings came earlier and earlier these days, even though the numbers on the clock registered the same from one day to the next. Even so, it just seemed harder for Elliana King to rouse herself, to kick off her covers and find a way to greet the world that was waiting for her just outside her front door.

It wasn't always this way, she thought sadly. There was a time that she felt sleeping was a waste of precious hours. Those were the days when she would bounce up long before the alarm's shrill bell officially went off, calling an end to any restful sleep she might have been engaged in.

But everything had changed two years ago.

These days, her dreams were sadly all empty, devoid of anything. The first year after Brett had been taken from her, she'd look forward to sleep because that was when he visited her. Every night, she dreamed of Brett, of the times they'd spent together, and it was as if she'd never lost him. All she had to do was close her eyes and within a few minutes, he was there. His smile, his voice, the touch of his hand. Everything.

She'd been more alive in sleep than while awake.

And then, just like that, he wasn't. Wasn't there no matter how hard she tried to summon him back. And getting up to face the day, face a life that no longer had Brett in it, became progressively harder for her.

Ellie sat up in bed, dragging her hand through blue-black hair Brett always referred to as *silky.* She was trying to dig up the will to actually put her feet on the floor and begin her day, a day that promised to be filled from one end to the other with nothing but ongoing work. Work that was meant to keep her busy and not thinking—not feeling.

Especially not feeling.

Work was her salvation—but first she had to get there.

Still trying to summon the energy to start, Ellie glanced at the nightstand on her left. The nightstand that held her phone, the lamp that was the first piece of furnishings Brett and she had chosen together—and the framed photograph of Brett wearing his uniform.

A ghost of a smile barely curved her lips as she reached out to touch the face that was looking back at her in the photograph.

And without warning, Ellie found herself blinking back tears.

"Still miss you," she murmured to the man who had been her whole world. She sighed and shook her head. "Almost wish I didn't," she told him because she had never been anything but truthful with Brett. "Because it hurts too much, loving you," she admitted.

Closing her eyes, Ellie pushed herself up off the bed, taking the first step into her day.

The other steps would come. Not easily, but at least easier. It was always that first step that was a killer, she thought, doing her best to get in gear.

She went through the rest of her morning routine by rote, hardly aware of what she was doing or how she got from point A to point B and so on. But she did, and eventually, Ellie was dressed and ready, standing at her front door, the consummate reporter prepared to undertake a full day of stories that needed to be engagingly framed for the public.

She knew how to put on a happy face for the camera.

No one except those who were very close to her—her mother; Jerry Ross, her cameraman; and maybe Marty Stern, the program manager who gave her her assignments—knew that she was always running on half-empty, because her reason for everything was no longer there.

Several times Ellie had toyed with the idea of just bowing out. Of not getting up, not going through the motions any longer. But she knew what that would do to her mother and she just couldn't do that to her, so she kept up the pretense. Her mother, widowed shortly before Brett had been killed, would be devastated if anything happened to her, so Ellie made sure nothing "happened" to her, made sure she kept putting one foot in front of the other.

And just kept going.

"But sometimes it's so hard," she admitted out loud

to the spirit of the man she felt was always with her even if she could no longer touch him.

Ellie took a deep breath as she opened the front door. It was fall and the weather was beautiful, as usual. "Another day in paradise," she murmured to herself.

Locking the door behind her, she forced herself to focus on what she had to do today—even though a very large part of her wanted to crawl back into bed and pull the covers up over her head.

"I know that look," Cecilia Parnell said the moment she sat down at the card table in Maizie's family room and took in her friend's face. "This isn't about playing cards, is it?"

Maizie was already seated and she was dealing out the cards. She raised an eyebrow in Cilia's direction and smiled.

"Not entirely," Maizie replied vaguely.

Theresa Manetti looked from Cilia to Maizie. She picked up the cards that Maizie had dealt her, but she didn't even bother fanning them out in her hand or looking at them. Cilia, Theresa knew, was right.

"Not at *all*," Theresa countered. "You've got a new case, don't you?" She did her best to contain her excitement. It had been a while now and she missed the thrill of bringing two soul mates together.

"You mean a new listing?" Maizie asked her innocently. "Yes, I just put up three new signs. As a matter of fact, there's one in your neighborhood, Theresa," she added.

"Oh, stop," Cilia begged, rolling her eyes. "You know that's not what Theresa and I are saying." She leaned closer over the small rectangular table that had seen so many of their card games over the years as well as borne witness to so many secrets that had been shared during that time. "Spill it. Male or female?"

"Female," Maizie replied. She smiled mysteriously. "Actually, you two know her."

Cilia and Theresa exchanged puzzled glances. "Personally?" Cilia asked.

Maizie raised a shoulder as if to indicate that she wasn't sure if they'd ever actually spoken with her friend's daughter.

"From TV."

Cilia, the more impatient one of the group, frowned. "We've been friends for over fifty years, Maizie. This isn't the time to start talking in riddles."

She supposed they were right. She didn't usually draw things out this way. Momentarily placing her own cards down, she looked at her friends as she told them, "It's Elliana King."

Theresa seemed surprised. "You mean the reporter on Channel—?"

Theresa didn't get a chance to mention the station. Maizie dispensed with that necessity by immediately cutting to the chase.

"Yes," she said with enthusiasm.

"She didn't actually come to you, did she?" Cilia asked in surprise.

"A girl that pretty shouldn't have any trouble—" Theresa began.

"No, no," Maizie answered, doing away with any further need for speculation. "Her mother did. Connie Williams," she told them for good measure. Both women were casually acquainted with Connie. "You remember," Maizie continued, "Ellie was the one who tragically found out on the air that her husband had been killed saving a couple being held up at gunpoint."

Theresa closed her eyes and shivered as she recalled the details. "I remember. I read that her station's ratings went through the roof while people watched that poor girl struggling to cope."

"That's the one," Maizie confirmed. "As I said, her mother is worried about her and wants us to find someone for Ellie."

"Tall order," Cilia commented, thinking that, given the trauma the young woman had gone through, it wasn't going to be easy.

"Brave woman," Maizie responded.

"No argument there," Theresa agreed.

Both women turned toward Cilia, who had gone strangely silent.

"Cilia?" Theresa asked, wondering what was going on in their friend's head.

Maizie zeroed in on what she believed was the cause of Cilia's uncharacteristic silence. Maizie was very proud of her gut instincts.

"You have something?" she asked.

Looking up, Cilia blinked as if she was coming out of deep thought.

"Maybe," she allowed. "One of the women who work for me was just telling me about her neighbor the other day. Actually," Cilia amended, "Olga was making a confession."

"Why?" Theresa asked, puzzled.

Maizie went to the heart of the matter. "What kind of a confession?" she pressed.

"She told me she offered to clean the young man's

apartment for free because it was in such a state of chaos," she explained. "And Olga felt she was betraying me somehow with that offer."

Theresa still wasn't sure she was clear about what was going on. "Why did she offer to clean his place? Was it like a trade agreement?" she asked. "She did something for him, then he did something for her?"

"It wasn't like that," Cilia quickly corrected, guessing at what her friend was inferring was behind the offer. "She told me that she felt sorry for the guy. He's a police detective who's suddenly become the guardian of his ten-year-old niece."

Maizie was instantly interested. "How did that happen?"

"His brother and sister-in-law were in this horrific skiing accident. Specifically, there was an avalanche and they were buried in it. By the time the rescuers could get to them, they were both dead," Cilia told her friends. "Apparently there's no other family to take care of the girl except for Olga's neighbor."

Theresa looked sufficiently impressed. "Sounds like a good man," she commented.

"Sounds like a man who could use a little help," Maizie interjected thoughtfully.

Maizie took off her glasses and gazed around the table at her friends. Ideas were rapidly forming and taking shape in her very fertile brain.

"Ladies," she announced with a smile, "we have homework to do."

"But I don't need a babysitter," Heather Benteen vehemently protested.

"I told you, kid, she's not a babysitter," Colin Benteen told his highly precious niece, a girl he'd known and loved since birth. Life had been a great deal easier when the only role he occupied was that of her friend, her coconspirator. This parenting thing definitely had a downside. "If you want to call her something, call her a *young-girl-sitter*," he told Heather, choosing his words carefully.

"I don't need one of those, either," Heather shot back. "I'll be perfectly fine coming home and doing my homework even if you're not here." She glared accusingly at her uncle, her eyes narrowing. "You don't trust me."

"I trust you," Colin countered with feeling.

Heather fisted her hands and dug them into her hips. "Then what's the problem?"

"The problem is," he told his niece patiently, "that I know the temptation that's out there." He gave her a knowing look. "I was just like you once."

"You were a ten-year-old girl?" Heather challenged.

"No, I was a ten-year-old boy, wise guy," he told her, affectionately tugging on one of her two thick braids. "Now, humor me. Olga offered to be here when you come home and hang around until I get off."

She tried again. "Look, Uncle Colin, I don't want to give you a hard time—"

"Then don't," he said, cutting Heather off as he grabbed a slice of toast.

Heather was obviously not going to give up easily. "I don't like having someone spy on me."

"Here's an idea," he proposed, taking his gun out of the lockbox on the bookshelf where he always deposited his weapon when he came home at night. "You can get your revenge by not doing anything noteworthy and boring her to death."

The preteen scowled at him. "So not the point," she insisted.

He wasn't about to get roped into a long philosophical discussion with his niece. She had to get to school and he needed to be at work.

"Exactly the point," he replied. "Olga will be here when I'm not, just as she has been these last few weeks—and we're lucky to have her. End of discussion," he told her firmly.

"For there to have been a discussion, I would have had to voice my side of it," she pointed out, all but scowling at him in a silent challenge that said she had yet to frame her argument.

Colin paused for a moment as he laughed and shook his head. "Sue me. I've never raised a ten-year-old before and I want to get this right."

The impatient look faded from her face and Heather smiled. She knew that they were both groping around in the dark, trying to find their way. Her uncle had always been very important to her, even before she'd woken up to find that the parameters of her world had suddenly changed so drastically.

She gave him a quick hug, as if she knew what was really on his mind. Concern. "We'll be all right, Uncle Colin."

"Yes, we will," he agreed. He pointed toward the front door. "Now let's go."

For the sake of pretense, Heather sighed dramatically and then marched right out of his ground-floor garden apartment.

* * *

Less than an hour later, Colin found himself halfway around the city, tackling a would-be art thief who was trying to make off with an original painting he'd stolen from someone's private collection in the more exclusive side of Bedford.

The call had gone out and he'd caught it quite by accident because his new morning route—he had to drop Heather off at school—now took him three miles out of his way and, as it so happened today, right into the path of the escaping art thief.

Waiting for the light to change, Colin saw a car streak by less than ten feet away from him. It matched the description that had come on over the precinct's two-way radio.

"Son of a gun," he muttered in disbelief. The guy had almost run him over. "Dispatch, I see the vehicle in question and I'm pursuing it now."

Turning his wheel sharply, he made a U-turn and proceeded to give chase. Despite his adrenaline pumping, he hated these chases, hated thinking of what was liable to happen if the utmost care as well as luck weren't at play here.

He held his breath even as he mentally crossed his fingers.

After a short time and some rather tricky, harrowing driving, he pursued the thief right into a storage-unit facility.

"You've got to be kidding me," he muttered under his breath. Did the guy actually believe he was going to lose him here? Talk about dumb moves...

He supposed he had to be grateful for that. Had the thief hit the open road, he might have lost him or someone might have gotten hit—possibly fatally—during the pursuit.

As it was, he managed to corner the man. Colin jumped out of his car and completed the chase on foot, congratulating himself that all those days at the gym paid off. He caught up to the thief, who had unintentionally led him not only to where he had planned on hiding this painting that he'd purloined but to a number of others that apparently had been stolen at some earlier date.

It took a moment to sink in. When it did, Colin tried not to let his jaw drop. Things like this didn't usually happen in Bedford, which, while not a sleepy little town, wasn't exactly a hotbed of crime, either.

"Wow, you've been quite the eager beaver, haven't you?" Colin remarked as he snapped a pair of handcuffs on the thief's wrists.

"Don't know what you're talking about," the thief declared. "Never saw these other paintings before in my life," he swore, disavowing any previous connection.

"And yet you came here to hide the one you stole this morning," Colin pointed out. "Small world, wouldn't you say?"

"I never saw these before!" the slight man repeated loudly.

Colin shook his head as he led the thief out to his waiting car. "Didn't your mama teach you not to lie?" he asked.

"I'm not saying another word without my lawyer," the thief announced, and dramatically closed his mouth.

"Good move," Colin said in approval. "Not much

left to say anyway, seeing as how all these paintings speak for themselves."

Desperate, the thief made one last attempt to move Colin as he was being put into the backseat. "Look, this is just a big misunderstanding."

"Uh-huh."

Panic had entered the man's face, making Colin wonder if he was working for someone else, someone he feared. "I can make it worth your while if you just look the other way, let me go. I'll leave the paintings. You can just tell everyone you found them."

Colin smiled to himself. It never ceased to amaze him just how dumb some people could be. "Maybe you should have thought of the consequences before you started putting this private collection together for yourself." He saw the thief opening his mouth and sensed there was just more of the same coming. "Too late now," he told the man.

With that, he took out his cell phone and called in to the station for backup to come and collect all the paintings. There were going to be a lot of happy art owners today, he mused. They wouldn't be reunited with their paintings immediately, since for now, the pieces were all being kept as evidence, but at least they knew the art had been recovered and was safe.

He glanced at his watch as he waited for his call to go through.

It was just nine thirty, he realized. Nine thirty on a Monday morning. His week was off and running.

Chapter Two

Maizie put as much stock in fate as the next person. She didn't, however, sit back and just assume that fate would step in and handle all the small details that were always involved in making things happen. That was up to her.

Which was why she was on the phone that morning calling Edward Blake, an old friend of her late husband's as well as a recent client she'd brought to Theresa's attention. The latter had involved Edward's youngest daughter, Sophia. Theresa had catered her wedding reception at less than her usual going rate.

Maizie used that as her opening when she placed her call to the news station's story director.

What had prompted her call was a story she heard on her radio as she was driving into work. The opportunity seemed too good to pass up. That, she felt, had been fate's part. The rest would require her help.

"Edward," she said cheerfully the moment she heard him respond on the other end of the line, "this is Maizie Sommers."

There was a pause, and then recognition set in. "Maizie, of course. How are you?"

"I'm well, thank you," she replied as if she had all the time in the world rather than what she assumed was a clock ticking the minutes away. She knew how the news world worked. "I just called to see how the newlyweds were doing."

"Fine, fine," Blake asserted in his booming baritone voice. "They're not looking for a house yet, though," he told her, obviously assuming that was why she was checking in with him.

"No, I wouldn't think so," she answered with a laugh. "It's much too early to start thinking about dealing with things like escrow and closing costs and homeowner associations." She paused for just a beat, then forged ahead. "But I did call to ask you a favor."

Their friendship dated back to the final year in college. Edward had been a friend of her late husband's. They had pulled all-nighters, helping each other study and pass final exams. "Name it."

"That news reporter you have working for you, Elliana King," Maizie began, then paused so that the woman's name sank in.

"Ah, yes, great girl, hardest worker I've ever had," the station manager testified fondly with feeling. "What about her?"

"I just heard about what could be a good human-interest story for your station and thought you could send the King girl to cover it."

"Go on," Blake encouraged, intrigued. He genuinely liked and respected Maizie and was open to anything she had to pass on.

"According to the news blurb, a police detective in Bedford chased down this supposedly small-time art thief and wound up uncovering an entire cache of paintings in a storage unit that had been stolen in the last eighteen months. I thought you might want to send someone down to the precinct to interview this detective." And then she played what she felt was her ace card in this little venture. "So little of the news we hear is upbeat these days."

"Don't I know it," Blake said with a sigh. And then he chuckled. "So you're passing on assignments to me now, Maizie?"

"Just this one, Edward."

There was more to this and he knew it. Moreover, he knew that Maizie knew he knew, but he played his line out slowly like a fisherman intent on reeling in an elusive catch than a station manager in a newsroom that moved sometimes faster than the speed of light. "And you think I should assign King to follow up on it."

"Absolutely," Maizie enthused, adding, "She has a nice way about her."

"Oh, I agree with you. She definitely has a rapport with her audience," Blake said. When he heard nothing more illuminating on the other end, he asked, "Okay, what's really going on, Maizie? Is this some kind of a matchmaking thing?"

"I have no idea what you mean, Edward," Maizie told him in far too innocent a voice.

"Right. Belinda told me what you and your friends are up to in your spare time," Blake said, referring to his wife. And then he became serious. "If you think you've found a way to get the pain out of King's eyes, go for it. You've got my vote."

Relieved that the man was so easily on board, Maizie tactfully pointed out, "What we need is your assignment, Edward."

"That, too. Okay, give me the details one more time," he instructed, pulling over a pad and pencil, two staples of his work desk that he absolutely refused to surrender no matter how many electronic gadgets littered his desk and his office. His defense was that a pad and pencil never failed.

"Don't get too comfortable," Jerry Ross warned Ellie just as she sank down behind her desk in the overly crowded newsroom.

The six-two onetime linebacker for a third-string minor-league football team strode over to the woman he followed around with his camera a good part of each day, sometimes successfully, sometimes only to see his footage ignobly die on the cutting room floor.

"Up and at 'em, Ellie," he coaxed. "We've got ourselves an assignment."

Ellie had just begun to sit down but instantly bounced back up to her feet again. She was more than ready to go wherever the assignment took them.

Two years ago it would have been because each story represented a fresh opportunity to put her stamp on something that was unfolding. Now it was because each story necessitated her having to abandon her private thoughts and focus on whatever the news report required from her. The first casualty was her social life, which she more than willingly surrendered. She really didn't have one to speak of now that Brett was no longer in her life.

"Where to?" Ellie asked.

Jerry held up the written directive he'd just received for them. "Blake wants us to do a story about this police detective at the police station."

"Blake?" she questioned, puzzled. She fell into step beside her cameraman as he went out of the building and to the parking lot where their news van was waiting for them. "You mean Marty, don't you?" Marty Stern was the one who handed out their assignments, not the station manager.

"No," Jerry insisted, "I mean Blake." It had struck him as odd as it did her, but he'd learned not to question things that came from on high. "This assignment came down from Edward Blake himself."

She hurried down the steps into the lot without even looking at them. "Why?"

Reaching the van, Jerry shrugged as he got in on the driver's side. He glanced over his shoulder to check that his equipment was where he had put it earlier. It was a nervous habit of his since there was no place else his camera and the rest of his gear could be. The cameraman always packed it into the van first thing on arrival each morning. But checking on its position was somehow comforting to him.

Satisfied that it was there, he turned forward again. "That's above my pay grade," he told her. "I'm just relating the message and telling you what he said he wanted."

After putting the key into the ignition, Jerry turned it and the van hummed to life.

"All I know is that this detective had just swung by Los Naranjos Elementary School to drop off his kid—a niece, I think Blake said—and he almost tripped over the thief. Who cut him off as he raced by." Jerry told her with disbelief. "Anyway, when the detective followed the guy, he wound up cornering him in a storage unit. Guess what else was in the storage unit."

Ellie was watching the cluster of residential streets pass by her side window. The tranquil scene wasn't even registering. She felt more tired than usual and it was hard for her to work up any enthusiasm for what she was hearing, even the fake kind.

"It's Monday, Jerry. I don't do guessing games until Tuesday," she told the cameraman as if it was a rule written somewhere.

Undaunted, Jerry continued his riveting edge-of-her-seat story. "The detective found a bunch of other paintings stored there that, it turns out, had been stolen over the last eighteen months. It's your favorite," the cameraman pointed out. "Namely, a happy-ending story."

"Not for the thief," Ellie murmured under her breath.

Jerry heard her. "That's not the lede Blake wants us to go with," he told her. "Turns out that this isn't this detective's first brush with being in the right place at the right time."

"Oh?" Ellie did her best to sound interested, but she was really having trouble raising her spirits this morning. She'd resigned herself to the fact that some mornings were just going to be worse than others and this was one of those mornings. She needed to work on that, Ellie told herself silently. Jerry didn't deserve to be sitting next to a morose woman.

Maybe coffee would help, she reasoned.

"Yeah," Jerry was saying as he navigated the streets, heading for the precinct. "I didn't get the details to that. Figure maybe you could do a follow-up when you do the interview."

She nodded absently, still not focused on the story. Out of sheer desperation, Ellie forced herself to make a few notes. Something had to spark her. "What's the detective's name?"

Jerry shrugged. "Blake said we're supposed to ask the desk sergeant to speak to the detective who uncovered the stolen paintings."

"In other words, you don't have a name," she concluded.

The curly-headed cameraman spared her an apologetic look. "Sorry. Blake seemed in a hurry for us to get there. Said the story had already been carried on the radio station. Wanted us there before another news station beat us to it."

Well, that was par for the course, Ellie thought. She sighed. "Why is it that every story is *the* story— until it's not?"

She received a wide, slightly gap-toothed smile in response. "Beats me. All I know is that all this competition is good for my paycheck. I've got a college tuition to fund."

"Jackie is only five," she reminded him, referring to the cameraman's only child.

Jerry nodded, acting as if she had made his point

for him. "Exactly. I can't let the grass grow beneath my feet."

Jerry stepped on the gas.

The police department was housed in a modern-looking building that was barely seven years old. Prior to that, the city's core had been domiciled in an old building that dated back to the '50s and had once contained farm supplies. People still called the present location the *new precinct*. Centrally located, it was less than five miles from the news station. They got there in no time flat, even though every light had been against them.

Ellie got out first, but Jerry's legs were longer and he reached the building's front entrance several strides ahead of her.

"Ladies first," the cameraman told her, holding the door open for Ellie.

She smiled as she passed him and headed straight for the desk sergeant's desk. She made sure she took out her credentials and showed them to the dour-faced man before she identified herself.

Even so, the desk sergeant, a snow-white-haired man whose shoulders had assumed a permanent slump, presumably from the weight of the job, took his time looking up at the duo.

The moment he did, Ellie began talking. "I'm Ellie King and this is my cameraman, Jerry Ross." She told him the name of her news studio, then explained, "We're here to interview one of your detectives."

White bushy eyebrows gathered together in what seemed to be a preset scowl as the desk sergeant squinted at her credentials.

"Any particular one?" he asked in a voice that was so low it sounded as if he was filtering it over rocks.

"Detective," he said a bit more loudly when she didn't answer his question. "You want to interview any particular one?" His voice did not become any friendlier as it grew in volume.

"The one who caught that art thief," Jerry answered, speaking up.

The desk sergeant, Sergeant Nolan according to the name plate on his desk, scowled just a tad less as he nodded. "You wanna talk to Benteen," he told them.

The moment Nolan said the name, it all but echoed inside her head.

It couldn't be, Ellie thought. *Breathe, Ellie, breathe!*

"Excuse me," she said out loud, feeling like someone in the middle of a trance. "Did you say Benteen?"

"Yeah. Detective Colin Benteen," the desk sergeant confirmed, acting as if each word he uttered had come from some private collection he was loath to share with invasive civilians. Nolan turned to look at a patrolman on his right. "Mallory, tell Benteen to come down here. There're some people here who want to talk to him."

Having sent the patrolman on his errand, the sergeant turned his attention to the people from the news station. "You two wait over there," he growled, pointing to an area by the front window that was empty. "And don't get in the way," he warned.

"Friendly man," Jerry commented, moving to the space that the sergeant had indicated. When he turned around to glance at Ellie, he saw that she'd suddenly gone very pale. A measure of concern entered his eyes. "You feeling all right, Ellie?"

"Yes," she responded. Her voice sounded hollow to her ears.

It was an automatic response, but the thing was that she *wasn't* all right. She'd recognized the name of the detective, and for a moment, everything had frozen within her. She tried to tell herself it was just an odd coincidence. Maybe it was just a relative. After all, Benteen wasn't *that* uncommon a name.

It had been a patrolman with that last name who had come to the scene of the robbery that had stolen Brett from her. This was a detective they were waiting for.

Because of the circumstances that had been involved and the fact that she had removed herself from the scene, Ellie had never actually met the policeman who had arrived shortly after Brett had foiled the robbery. The patrolman, she was later told, who'd tried—and failed—to save Brett's life.

But she knew his name and at the time had promised herself that as soon as she was up to it, she would seek out this Officer Benteen and thank him for what he had tried to do—even if he had ultimately failed.

But a day had turned into a week and a week had turned into a month.

After several of those had passed, she gave up the notion of finding the policeman to thank him for his efforts.

After a while, the thought of talking to the man who had watched Brett's life ebb away only brought back the scene to her in vivid colors. A scene she was still trying, even at this point, to come to grips with. She honestly didn't think that she was up to it. So eventually she avoided pursuing the man altogether.

Jerry was watching her with concern. "You don't look fine. If I didn't know any better, I'd say that you look like you're about to break into a cold sweat."

"Jerry, I already have a mother," she told him, an annoyed edge in her voice—she didn't like being read so easily. "I said I'm fine."

He was not convinced and was about to say as much when she turned away from him and toward the man she saw walking toward them. The expression on her face had Jerry turning, as well. If anything, she appeared even paler than she had a moment ago.

"You look like you're seeing a ghost," he remarked uneasily.

The universe was sending her a message, she thought. It was time to tie up this loose end.

"Not a ghost," she answered. "Just someone I never got to thank properly."

The moment she said that, Jerry knew. The name the desk sergeant had said had been nagging at him. He knew it from somewhere…

"Oh God, you mean that's him?" Jerry cried. "The policeman who…?"

She waved the cameraman into silence, her attention fully focused on the tall, athletic-looking man in the navy jacket, gray shirt and jeans who was walking toward them.

He had a confident walk, she noted, like someone who felt he had the angels on his side. Maybe he did, she thought.

Ellie unconsciously squared her shoulders as the detective drew closer.

It was time to make up for her omission. The only thing that was left to decide was whether she would do it before they began the interview so she could get it out of the way or wait until after the interview was over so that it wouldn't make the man feel awkward or uncomfortable. Viewers were always quick to pick up on awkwardness and she didn't want to cause the detective any undue discomfort. It didn't make for a good segment, and after all, wasn't that why she was here?

Ellie made up her mind. The information as to who they were to one another could wait until after she finished talking to him, for the benefit of the home audience.

It took a great deal of effort for her, but by now she was used to playing a part.

Ellie forced a welcoming smile to her face and put out her hand to the detective as he came forward. Her entire attention was now on making the hero of the moment feel comfortable.

"Hi," she greeted him. "I'm Ellie and this is Jerry, and we'd like to ask you a few questions about those paintings you uncovered."

Chapter Three

The woman standing by the front window next to the pleasant-faced hulk with the unruly hair was cute.

Beyond cute, Colin amended. There was something appealing about her that he couldn't quite put his finger on. As best as he could analyze it, he sensed an intriguing combination of sadness mixed with an undercurrent of energy radiating from her.

And, more startling and thus far more important, he realized that for the first time in months, he found himself both attracted and interested.

There'd been a time when his older brother, Ryan, had called him a ladies' man, a "babe magnet" and a number of less flattering but equally descriptive terms. And at the time, they had all been rather accurate.

But all that had been before life had abruptly changed for him. Before his brother and sister-in-law, Jennifer, had been involved in that freak skiing accident that had resulted in their being swallowed up by an avalanche. Who could have predicted this outcome when Ryan and Jennifer had gone on a last-minute spur-of-the-moment vacation because a late-season unexpected snowfall had occurred and they were both avid skiers?

Just like that, in the blink of an eye, he suddenly found himself the only family that their only daughter, Heather, had left.

His personality, not to mention his priorities, had changed overnight. He hadn't been on so much as a date since he'd had to fly to Aspen to identify Ryan and Jennifer's bodies and to pick up his niece. Heather had been in bed asleep when it had all happened. Her parents had opted to sneak in a quick early-morning ski run before she woke up—not thinking that it would be the last thing that they would ever do.

Stunned, Colin had never thought twice about assuming this new responsibility. He turned his entire life around, then and there, vowing that Heather would always come first.

He couldn't give up what he did for a living—he'd worked too hard to get to where he was. It came with its own set of dangers, and that couldn't be helped. But he could definitely make sure that any time outside his job would go to being with Heather, to making sure that she wouldn't be permanently scarred by the loss of her parents. He'd vowed that he would always be there when Heather needed him to make the night terrors go away.

But just for a moment, this petite woman standing before him took Colin back to the man he had been before all of this had happened to change his life. It made him remember just how he'd felt when a really attractive woman crossed his path.

"Detective?" Ellie prodded when he didn't seem to have heard her, or at least wasn't attempting to respond to her greeting.

"Sorry," Colin apologized, rousing himself out of the temporary mental revelry he'd fallen into. He flashed a smile at her that one of his former girlfriends had called "naturally sexy." "I got distracted for a moment."

She was about to ask him if it was because he recalled who she was, but then she remembered that she had given him only her first name. Even if she'd told him her full name, that wouldn't necessarily mean that the detective would remember her husband and that fatal night at the convenience store.

Or even if he did recall every moment of that night, there was no reason to believe that he would make the connection between her and the man he couldn't save. King was, after all, a common enough name. Most likely, Benteen probably hadn't even gotten Brett's name after everything had gone back to normal—or as normal as it could have gone back to, she silently corrected.

No, if the detective was distracted on her account, he was probably trying to place where he'd seen her before.

As if the presence of a cameraman wasn't enough of a clue, she thought wryly.

"No problem," Ellie told the detective. In her opinion, that was a throwaway line that blanketed a lot of territory. She just wanted to do this story and move on. "Your CO told us we could take up a little of your time and ask you about the huge coup you just scored."

Colin looked at her puzzled, not quite following the sexy reporter. "Excuse me?"

"The paintings," Ellie prompted. "The stolen paintings that were in the storage unit you found."

Colin nodded in response but said nothing.

"Well?" she asked, waiting for him to start speaking. Talk about having to pull words out of someone's mouth. The detective was either exceptionally modest or exceedingly camera shy.

"That about covers it," he told her.

She could see by the look that Jerry gave her that he had the same thought as she did. This wasn't going to film well, not unless she could find a way to make this detective come around and start talking. She had a feeling that he would engage the audience once he got comfortable.

"You're being modest," she said, her voice coaxing him to elaborate.

He surprised her by saying, "Bragging rights aren't a part of this job."

Okay, she thought. He *did* need to be coaxed. A lot. She had to admit that this wasn't what she'd expected. Some people, once they got in front of a camera, wouldn't stop talking. This one seemed reluctant to even start.

"Still, I'm sure that it's not every police detective who gets to take down an art thief who's been plaguing the city."

"I really can't take any kind of credit for what happened. It's not as if this was the result of long hours of planning." He shrugged. "This was all actually just a big accident," Colin told her.

The job had made her somewhat cynical. It wasn't anything that she was particularly proud of, just a fact. But Ellie was beginning to believe that the detective was being serious. He was the genuine article. And because of this, she found herself trying to reach out to Benteen.

"There's that modesty again," she said. "I tell you what—why don't you walk me through exactly what happened and we'll go from there?"

She could see by the look on the detective's face that he was about to dismiss the whole incident. It made him a rare find in her book. Most men couldn't stop talking about themselves. But the station manager obviously was expecting a story and she wasn't about to come back empty-handed. It wasn't advisable.

"Word for word," Ellie urged again. "Paint a picture for me, so to speak."

Colin glared at the camera in Jerry's hands. It was clearly the enemy. "Are you going to film this?"

"That is the idea," Ellie said breezily. "Jerry's just going to keep on filming and when we're done, it'll be edited down to about a minute of airtime. Two, tops," she promised. She could see that the detective was wavering. All he needed was a little push that would send him over to her side. She felt she had just the thing. "You get final say on the footage."

"I do?" Colin asked, not entirely certain that she was on the level. He was aware of how badly some of his fellow detectives had been portrayed to the public. He wanted no part of that.

"Maybe this'll convince you," she said, trying again.

"Your CO signed off on this because he knew this would create a positive image of the Bedford PD. And my station manager thought this would be a feel-good piece that would really go over well, especially since those pieces are so few and far between."

"Well, I guess I'm sold, then," Colin told her. What he was sold on, he admitted, was the way her clear blue eyes seemed to sparkle as she tried to convince him. That alone was worth the price of admission.

Ellie smiled at the detective.

"Good." She glanced over her shoulder to make sure that Jerry had the camera in position. He did. "All right, just tell me what happened."

"Tell you?" he asked, thinking he was supposed to talk to the camera.

"Just me," she assured him. "Talk to *me*."

That made it easier. She had a face that invited conversation—as well as a number of other stray thoughts. "I'd just dropped off my niece, Heather, at school—"

Her ears instantly perked up. "Is that a usual thing for you?" The man was beginning to sound like a Boy Scout.

"It is ever since I became her sole guardian," Colin answered matter-of-factly.

As a human-interest story, this was just getting better and better, Ellie thought. She made a mental note to ask him more questions regarding that situation so she could annotate her commentary once the film had been edited.

"Go on," she urged.

"An APB came on over the two-way radio about a

B and E that had just gone down less than three blocks away from Heather's school," he said.

She wanted to get back to that, but first she wanted him to explain some of the terminology he'd just used. "An APB and B and E?" she asked, waiting for him to spell the words out. She knew what he was saying, but the audience might not.

"*All points bulletin* and *breaking and entering*," the detective explained. He was so used to those terms and others being tossed around that it didn't occur to him that someone might not know what he was talking about.

"Okay. Go on," she said, smiling at him.

It was a smile he caught himself thinking he could follow to the ends of the earth.

But not anymore, remember?

"The homeowner called 911 to say that he'd heard a noise and when he woke up, he saw a man running across his lawn carrying off his painting. Apparently, the thief had broken in while the guy was still asleep."

She nodded, focusing on the image of a thief dashing across a lawn with a stolen painting clutched in his hands.

"Definitely not something you see every day," Ellie agreed drolly.

Colin nodded. "That's when I saw this guy driving a van that matched the description dispatch had put out. So I followed him. Turns out it wasn't all that far away," he added. "He took the painting to a local storage unit. As I watched him, he stashed the painting he'd just stolen in an ordinary storage unit. When I came up behind him, I saw that he had what amounted to fifteen other paintings inside the unit."

Colin paused in his narrative to tell her, "There've been a rash of paintings stolen in Bedford in the last eighteen months."

She looked at him, waiting for more. When he didn't continue or make any attempt to brag, she asked, "And the paintings that you saw, were they the ones that had been stolen?"

He nodded. "One and the same."

She tried to get more details. "Was this guy part of a gang?"

"Not from anything that I could ascertain," Colin told her. "When I questioned him, he said he had taken all the paintings. I think he was telling the truth."

"And he hadn't tried to fence any of them?" she asked. It didn't seem possible.

Colin laughed softly. "Turns out that the guy just likes works of art and he didn't have the money to buy any of his own, so he came up with this plan." Colin shrugged. "Takes all kinds," was his comment.

It certainly did, Ellie silently agreed. "That almost sounds too easy," she said.

"I know," he replied. "But sometimes everything just falls into place at the right time and the right way. It doesn't happen often," Colin allowed. "But it does happen."

"Well, apparently, it did for you," Ellie observed. She all but expected to see the detective kick the dust and murmur, "Ah, shucks."

Colin turned out not to be as clueless as she momentarily thought him to be. A knowing smile curved his mouth as he guessed, "You're not convinced."

The smile came of its own volition. "It's my doubting-Thomas side," she admitted.

"We're checking the guy for priors," Colin told her. "Right now he's clean, but we're not finished. I could give you an update later," he offered.

"I would appreciate it," she said, then turned toward something that she knew would interest her viewers. "Tell me more about your niece. How long have you been her guardian?"

The question caught him off guard. They were just talking about the thief's lack of priors. "Is that important?" he asked, unclear as to why it should be, especially in this context.

If nothing else, Ellie knew her audience and how to make a story appealing to them. "The viewers love to hear details like that about selfless heroes."

"I'm not a hero and I'm not selfless," he told her, his manner saying that he wasn't just mouthing platitudes or what he felt passed for just the right amount of humility. His tone told Ellie that this detective was being straightforward with her, which she had to admit impressed her. He could have just as easily allowed her to build him up without protest.

"Why don't we leave that to the viewer to decide?" Ellie suggested. "Now, how long have you been your niece's guardian?"

"Six months," he told her.

Again, he didn't elaborate or tell her any more than the bare minimum. Was he being modest? Or was that a highly developed sense of privacy taking over?

Either way, her job was to push the boundaries a little in order to get him to open up. "What happened?" she asked.

He didn't look annoyed, but he did ask, "Is this really necessary?"

She was honest with him, sensing that the detective would appreciate it. "For the story? No. This is just me asking."

That brought up another host of questions in his mind. "Why?"

She wanted him to trust her. She needed to know the kind of man her husband had spent the last seconds of his life with. Only then would she know if he had done all that he could to try to save Brett. She was aware that he had probably said he had and filled out a report to that effect, but she wanted to be convinced.

"Shut off the camera, Jerry," she said, glancing over her shoulder at her cameraman. "We've got our story. I'll meet you at the van."

Jerry looked at her skeptically, still worried about her. She hadn't told the detective of their connection yet, but that didn't mean she wasn't going to, and when she did, she might need someone there for her.

But he couldn't say anything, because it wasn't his place. And if he did say anything, he knew that Ellie would *put* him in his place because she refused to tolerate anything remotely resembling pity, even if it came in the guise of sympathy.

All he could do was ask, "Are you sure?"

"I'm sure." The words *Now go* were implied if not said out loud.

Shaking his head, Jerry took his camera and walked out.

"See you around, Detective," he said by way of a parting comment.

Turning back to the detective, Ellie picked up the conversation where she'd left it. "You asked me why before."

Colin had just assumed that she'd forgotten and would go off on another topic. That she didn't raised his estimation of her. And he really had to say that so far, he liked what he saw. Liked it a lot. Maybe there was hope for him yet. At least, he'd like to think so.

"Yes, I did." His tone gave her an opening to continue her line of thinking.

"Because I am one of those people who has to know everything," she told him simply. "That doesn't mean I repeat everything I hear or everything I know, but I *need* to know it. And once I have all the information and can process it, then I can move on."

He looked at her and made a judgment call. "So this really isn't for your 'story'?" he asked.

"No. Not directly." And then she qualified her statement. "That doesn't mean that I won't use a piece of what you tell me—but again, we'll run it by you first. You'll get the final okay."

He had to admit that he thought it a generous way to proceed. "Is this your normal procedure?"

Ellie laughed. She had no idea that he found the sound captivating. "There is no such thing as 'normal' procedure. It is what it is at the moment."

Colin paused, considering her words and if he believed her.

Like a lot of true dyed-in-the-wool detectives, he had "gut feelings."

"Gut feelings" that saw him through a lot and, on occasion, kept him safe. His gut feeling told him that the woman with the deep crystal-blue eyes was telling him the truth.

He took a chance. "They died in an avalanche."

"That had to be terrible for you," she said. It was

certainly different from the usual car crash or drive-by shooting. She managed to control her reaction so he wasn't aware that what he said had affected her.

"It wasn't exactly a walk in the park for Heather, either," he pointed out.

"You were the one who broke the news to her?" Even as Ellie asked the question, she knew that he would have taken it upon himself to tell his niece. Benteen struck her as that sort of person. She was filled with empathy for both the detective and his niece, knowing what being told news like that felt like.

"I wasn't about to let anyone else do it," he said.

No, I wouldn't have thought so.

Without her realizing it, her estimation of the detective rose up yet another notch.

Chapter Four

Jerry appeared to be dozing in the news van, but he snapped to attention the moment the passenger-side door opened.

"So, how did he take it?" the cameraman asked her.

"Take it?" Ellie repeated absently as she climbed into the van. After closing the door, she pulled on her seat belt and snapped it into place.

Jerry watched her intently for a moment. "You didn't tell him that he was there the night your husband died, did you?"

Ellie shrugged, settling into her seat. "I didn't get an opportunity." She avoided looking at Jerry as she said, "The timing wasn't right."

Jerry turned his key, starting up the van. For an instant, the music he'd had playing on the radio stopped, then resumed. Someone was singing about surviving.

"This isn't the game-winning pitch to home plate we're talking about, Ellie. Don't you think the good detective should know that he tried to save the husband of the woman who was interviewing him?"

"I don't see how that would make any difference to this story," she countered stubbornly.

"No," Jerry allowed, "but it might make a difference to him."

There was a measure of defiance in Ellie's eyes as she turned them on Jerry.

"Why? I'm going to treat him fairly. We've got nothing but glowing words for him in this spot. His CO seemed pretty high on him and I'm sure if we interview a couple of the people whose paintings were recovered, they'll talk about him like he's their patron saint come to earth."

Jerry sighed as he barreled through a yellow light before it turned red, narrowly missing cutting off a tan SUV.

"He's a good guy, yes, I get that. But that doesn't change the fact that you should tell him about your connection," he insisted.

She didn't see what good it would do and telling Benteen would force her to relive a night she couldn't seem to permanently bury.

"Why?" she challenged.

Jerry gave her a look. "Because you shouldn't be keeping it from him."

She didn't normally get annoyed, but "normal" was no longer part of her daily life.

"How did I get to be the bad guy in this?" she asked.

"You're not," Jerry told her in a voice that was much

lower than hers, "but if you don't tell him, this is going to be something that'll just fester between you and him—until it finally comes out. Think how uncomfortable you'll feel then."

"Well, it's not like we're going to be working together or we're a couple," she pointed out impatiently. "Once the story airs, we probably won't ever even run into one another."

The funny thing was, Ellie thought, that the detective was just the kind of man her mother would have picked out for her once upon a time. There was a lot about him that reminded her of Brett.

The next moment, she shut all those thoughts down. "For now," she said, addressing the point that Jerry had raised, "let's just say that maybe I didn't want to make *him* feel uncomfortable."

"Is that it?" Jerry asked. "Or is it that you just want to hold something back and maybe, oh, I don't know, spring it on him later?"

Why in heaven's name would she want to do that? Ellie shook her head.

"I think that you've been watching too many procedurals, Jerry," she told him.

The light turned red, forcing Jerry to come to a stop and allowing him to really stare at her as he said, "No, it's just that I care about you."

"Do me a favor. Care a little less," she requested. "I can take care of myself."

Jerry frowned. The light turned green and he hit the gas again. "I'm not so sure about that."

What had gotten into him? Jerry had always been her chief supporter. "What's that supposed to mean?"

"It's just that sometimes I get the feeling that you're

just sleepwalking through life, that you've decided to check out."

He pulled into a parking spot but made no effort to get out. He'd faithfully followed her around and they made a great team, but she wasn't about to hold on to him against his will.

"Are you telling me that you want to switch news reporters?" she asked suddenly. "Because if you do, I'm not going to stand in your way."

"No, I *don't* want to switch reporters." He frowned. "You know, you never used to be this touchy."

"Things change," she said vaguely.

His eyes narrowed as they bore right into her. "Do they?"

"Okay, now you're really beginning to sound like my mother, and while I really love her, I do *not* need two of her," she informed him, one hand on the car's doorknob. "You heard me. Once the piece you got today is edited, I did promise Detective Benteen that we'd let him have the final okay. When he does okay it, *then* I'll tell him. Does that meet with your approval?" she asked.

She realized that she was being short-tempered with Jerry because she knew he was right. But at the same time, she didn't want to go there, didn't want to revisit the pain that went with all that.

"You don't need my approval, Ellie."

"No," she told him pointedly, agreeing. "I don't. I also don't need you glaring at me, either."

"I'm not glaring," he protested. "I was just looking at you. The rest is in your head."

Ellie sighed. "How does your wife put up with you, anyway?" she asked as the tension began to drain from her. She'd overreacted and she knew it. Now all she wanted to do was just forget about it and get this piece in to the editor.

Jerry laughed. "Betsy worships the ground I walk on—you know that."

"Uh-huh," she murmured, getting out of the van. "Let's go get some of our background material for this story."

Jerry got out on his side, taking his faithful camera with him. "Your wish is my command."

Ellie spared him a glance as she rolled her eyes. "If only…"

Colin sighed. It had been a long, long day.

After his morning had started out with all four burners going, what with the lucky catch of that thief and his cache and then that knockout news reporter coming to ask him questions, his afternoon had turned into a slow-moving turtle, surrounding him with a massive collection of never-ending paperwork. Paperwork that he'd neglected far too long.

The trouble with ignoring paperwork was that it didn't go away; it just seemed to sit in dark corners and multiply until it became an overwhelming stack that refused to be ignored. Unfortunately, he'd reached that point today. He supposed it was a way to keep him humble, even though he wasn't given to grappling with a large ego. Philosophically, he'd rolled up his sleeves because he knew he had to do something to at least whittle down the pile a little before it smothered him.

Rather than begin at the beginning, which might have been the orderly thing to do, Colin decided to start with the most recent file since that case had been the one that brought the reporter into his life.

Besides, there was nothing like the feeling that came from actually being able to close a case rather than having it linger on indefinitely, doggedly haunting him because he hadn't been able to solve it.

What he especially liked about this last case—other than the fact that it had introduced him to the sexy reporter—was that the thief had been taken down, so to speak, without his having to fire a single shot. Not all cases involving robbery ended so peacefully.

More often than not, someone was hurt, sometimes fatally. Colin didn't admit it out loud, but he took it hard when that happened. It wasn't that he thought of himself as some kind of superhero who should be able to prevent things like that from happening. He didn't think of himself as a hero at all, but the fact that he wasn't able to prevent a fatality really ate away at him for a long time.

Maybe that was why before Heather had become his responsibility, he had lived a faster life, determined to enjoy himself as much as possible. Partly because life was short and could end at any time and partially to erase certain images from his mind.

Images like having a would-be hero's blood pool through the fingers of his hand as he desperately tried to stem the flow, desperately tried to keep the man alive. But he'd come on the scene just minutes too late. Too late to stop the gunman from firing that lethal shot, but at least not too late to take the gunman down.

It still kept him up at night sometimes or disturbed his dreams, intruding like an uninvited, unwanted visitor determined to disrupt everything. Those were the nights when Heather came into his bedroom to wake *him* up instead of the other way around.

They were a pair, he and Heather. Both trying to act as if nothing bothered them. She was becoming more like him each day, he realized, wondering how Ryan would have reacted to that little piece of news.

He found himself wishing Ryan was around to react to *anything*.

Colin rotated his shoulders, then just got up from his desk altogether. There was only so much sitting at a computer, inputting information, that a man could be expected to do.

He needed to get some air, he decided.

"See another art thief darting by?" Marconi, another detective sitting close by, asked as he looked up to see him walking out.

Colin took the remark in stride. "Very funny. I need to stretch my legs."

"Hey, Benteen, so when do we get to see that chiseled profile on TV?" another detective, Al Sanchez, asked, speaking up.

Colin merely shrugged. That alluring reporter had said she'd get back to him, but she hadn't mentioned when. "Beats me."

"I've been here fourteen years. Never had anyone come and film me," Marconi pretended to complain.

Sanchez ventured a theory. "Maybe they didn't want to risk their cameras breaking filming that ugly mug of yours."

Colin knew they didn't mean anything by it, but he ignored them anyway. The truth was that he really wasn't comfortable about being on camera. He'd been just doing his job and saw no reason for something like that to make the six-o'clock news—or whatever time it was going to be on.

Leaving the squad room, he shoved his hands into his pockets. His right hand came in contact with the card that the news reporter had given him just before she'd left.

He felt it for a moment, his fingers passing over the embossed lettering. Taking it out, he looked at the card for a long moment.

Elliana King.

Her number was written directly under that. Probably not hers, he discounted. Most likely, it was the studio number. Even so, for a moment, he was tempted to call it. But then he thought better of it. What was he going to say? "Hi, remember me? Would you like to get some coffee somewhere?"

That wasn't going to get him anywhere. She probably had her share of guys calling her. Besides, he didn't have time for things like that. He had Heather to look out for.

Colin put the card back into his pocket and just kept on walking.

Hours later, he finally unlocked the front door of his apartment. The moment he walked in, Olga Pavlova, his next-door neighbor, gathered together her things and headed straight for the door.

"Good evening, Detective," the woman said, nodding at him as she passed. And without another word, she was gone.

Which left just him and Heather. His niece was planted on the sofa in front of the wide-screen TV.

"You're watching the news?" he questioned.

"Olga says I need to be aware of the world around me. 'Is good to know,'" Heather said, doing a decent imitation of the woman's thick Russian accent.

"So how was your day?" Colin asked as he slid down next to Heather, loosening his tie as he went down.

Heather spared him a look. "I learned stuff, forgot stuff, the usual." And then she tossed the ball back into his court. "You?"

He would have rather spent twelve hours on his feet investigating a case than sitting at his desk for six battling paperwork.

"Mostly forgot stuff," he told her. He glanced at his watch. It was after six. "Did you have dinner?"

"Yeah." Her eyes were back on the screen, devouring everything she saw. "Olga brought over a casserole. She said to tell you it's in the refrigerator. It's in the refrigerator."

He laughed as he got up again. "Thanks, kid," Colin said, kissing the top of her head. "I knew I could count on you."

Colin was halfway to the kitchen when he heard Heather suddenly scream. In hindsight, it was more of a squeal, but at the time, he wasn't differentiating. He pivoted on his heel and raced back into the living room.

"What's wrong?" Colin asked, alert and looking in all directions at once. Heather wasn't the type to scream under normal circumstances. Something had either set her off or frightened her.

"Look!" Heather cried, pointing to the TV. "It's you!"

The words were partially muffled because she had

her hands over her mouth in utter surprise even as she talked. "You're on TV." Her head appeared to almost swivel as she looked from the image on the screen to her uncle and then back again. Her eyes were huge as she took in his TV image. "You didn't tell me you were on TV!"

"I didn't know," he answered, staring at the screen. The interview he'd given Ellie King this morning was being run on the evening news. "I mean, I wasn't supposed to be until I gave my final approval."

Heather had scrambled up to her knees and was staring at the image as if she had never seen her uncle before. She hardly heard him.

"You didn't tell me you met Ellie King." It was almost an accusation, as if he had kept a vital piece of information from her. "You *know* her?" she cried in complete wonder.

"No." But that wasn't entirely true. "I mean, not until this morning."

And just like that, the piece they were watching on the air was over.

"Where's the remote?" he asked Heather.

"I don't know. It was here," she said, distracted. The remote was barely on her radar. "Can I meet her?"

He was focused on finding the elusive remote. He pushed the cushions around until he finally found what he was looking for half buried under the last cushion. He extracted it, then pointed the device at the set as he pressed the rewind button.

Images did an awkward dance, moving backward until he got to the beginning of the piece.

"Meet who?" he finally asked, still looking at the TV monitor.

"Ellie King," Heather told him impatiently. "Can I meet her?"

Bringing the woman around for introductions was the last thing on his mind right now. He was annoyed, not because his vanity had been offended but because she'd lied to him. He hated being lied to.

"We'll see."

"Please, Uncle Colin," Heather begged. "She's just everything I want to be. Pretty and smart and she gets to do all these really great stories—"

Heather abruptly fell silent as the interview began from the beginning again.

Colin winced as he watched himself. He supposed that it wasn't as bad as he'd thought it was, but it still made him feel awkward. And he was still annoyed.

He didn't wait for the end of the piece this time. He tossed the remote back on the sofa next to Heather.

Taking the card that the reporter had given him out of his pocket, he pulled his cell phone out of his other pocket and proceeded to dial the number on the card.

He was bracing himself for an ordeal. He figured that he was going to have to verbally strong-arm his way to getting someone to either put Ellie King on the line or give him her number. He wasn't about to hang up without getting either satisfaction or the number.

Having worked himself up, Colin wasn't prepared to hear her voice.

"This is Ellie King. May I help you?" When no one responded, she said, "Hello, is anyone there?"

"This is Detective Benteen," Colin said, finally finding his voice.

She hadn't expected to hear from him so soon, but she should have known. The man had struck her as being on top of things. She knew he was calling about the segment they'd just aired.

She decided to get ahead of this before he tried to run her over. "Hello, Detective. We had to air your segment tonight."

"Had to?" he questioned.

She didn't really owe him an explanation. After all, he was a public servant and this had been done in the service of the public. The public had a right to know. But she had made him a promise, so she felt the need to explain why she'd gone back on it.

"I know I promised that you'd have the final say, but I've got people I answer to and they insisted that the segment go on tonight as is. It turned out pretty well, I thought." She crossed her fingers that he saw it that way, too.

"You lied to me." It wasn't an accusation but a flat statement. It carried with it not anger but a note of genuine disappointment. And that made her feel worse than if he'd launched into a tirade.

"I didn't lie," she replied. "I had every intention of showing you the clip first." When he said nothing, she felt uncomfortable, despite the fact that this ultimately wasn't really her fault. "The station manager wanted to air it before the other stations got it. I'm sorry, but these things happen. Listen, if you want me to make it up to you—" she began, not really certain where this would ultimately go.

He cut her short with two words. "I do."

Chapter Five

I do.

The detective's words echoed in her head for a moment.

Okay, what had she just gotten herself into, Ellie wondered. She really hadn't expected the man on the other end of the line to take her up on her offer, especially since it was so vague. Now she had no idea what to say to solidify the offer—or more accurately, to rescind it, which was what she really wanted to do.

But since she had made the offer and the detective had said yes, she had no choice but to at least hear him out and find out what he had in mind. She could always say no.

Taking a breath, Ellie did her best to sound cheerful as she asked, "How?"

"Do you remember that niece I mentioned when you interviewed me?"

His voice seemed to rumble against her ear, like the sound of thunder. She could feel it reverberating within her chest.

"Yes, I remember," Ellie said uncertainly.

Colin was watching Heather out of the corner of his eye. She was on her knees on the sofa and it seemed as if his niece had frozen in midmovement, completely riveted to the conversation he was having with the reporter she so obviously idolized.

Giving Heather an encouraging smile, he told Ellie, "She'd like to meet you."

"Oh?" Was that all? Ellie felt a flood of relief. She hadn't exactly known what to expect, but life had taught her these last two years always to expect the worst. This was definitely not the worst, not even close. "Sure, that would be very nice," she told him. "Where and when?"

"Well, considering the fact that we both have busy careers and Heather has school, how about sometime this weekend? Is that doable for you?" He'd anticipated some sort of in-depth negotiation. This was turning out to be easier than he'd thought. Maybe the gorgeous reporter did have a really nice side to her after all.

Ellie paused, doing a quick review in her head. So far, she had nothing planned for the weekend. "I'm not sure I can bring you and her around the studio for a tour this weekend—"

Now that he had put it out there and saw the hopeful look on Heather's face, he wasn't about to accept a rejection. "Then how about coming over to my place?"

The moment the words were out of his mouth, he

realized that sounded like a come-on and far too intimate for an innocent meeting. She'd think it was a ploy on his part—and maybe at one time, it might have been. But this was for Heather and he wasn't about to disappoint his niece if he could help it. This was the first time he'd seen the girl excited about anything since she'd come to live with him.

"Or we could meet you at a coffee shop," Colin suggested.

"Didn't you say she was ten? Isn't that a little young for coffee?" Ellie asked, wondering if the detective was telling her the truth—or if he had something else in mind by way of her making up for the unapproved aired segment.

"Yes, she's ten, but Heather has an old soul. Besides, this coffee shop serves hot chocolate, as well." Thinking the woman probably preferred everything on her terms, he told her, "Or you choose the location if my picking one makes you uncomfortable."

Was he insinuating that she was afraid to meet him? Half a dozen half-formed thoughts crowded her head extrapolating on that.

Ellie suppressed a sigh. She really missed the days when things were simpler and more transparent.

"A coffee shop is fine," she told him. "Name the place and the time. If I'm not on a story, I'll be there."

She was giving herself an out, Colin thought. He supposed he could appreciate that. But his foremost thought was of Heather, not the dark-haired reporter with the killer legs.

"And if you are?" he asked.

"Then I'll call—and reschedule," Ellie said simply.

"Sounds reasonable," Colin replied. "How does Saturday, ten o'clock, at Josie's Café sound?" he asked.

"Reasonable," Ellie said, using the same word he just had.

He began to give her the café's address and only got partway through.

"I know where it is," Ellie told him.

"Great. Then we'll see you then—barring rescheduling," Colin added for the woman's benefit.

Sensing that the next sound she was going to hear was the call being terminated, Ellie said, "Wait."

"Something else?" Colin asked.

She was probably going to regret this, Ellie thought, but she asked the question anyway. "What did you think of it?"

"You mean the segment you aired without my okay?"

She wasn't about to apologize again. She'd already told him why she'd had to go ahead with it, so she just skipped over that and went directly to her answer. "Yes. The segment—what did you think of it?"

Colin paused, then told her, "You look good on camera."

His answer caught her off guard. For just one second, she wondered if he really thought that. The next second, she shut the thought away, telling herself that didn't matter one way or another. She wanted to get his reaction to the segment.

"That's not what I'm asking and you know it. I'm asking if you liked the segment." Not waiting for an answer, she quickly emphasized, "I didn't misrepresent you or trivialize you. Actually, I think you came off quite heroically. As a matter of fact, I'd be surprised if this piece doesn't get you a few groupies."

When she'd watched the segment as it aired, she'd caught herself thinking he came off rather compelling as well as damn good-looking. Everything that was required by a hero of the moment.

"I'm not interested in groupies," he told her, dismissing her comment.

She really found that difficult to believe, given his age and his looks. Ellie decided to push that a little. Whether she was playing devil's advocate or trying to see just how genuine this detective was, she wasn't all that sure. She knew only that she wanted to hear Colin's answer, for reasons that she wasn't making clear to herself.

"A good-looking man like you?" she scoffed. "I find that very difficult to believe."

"Maybe in another life, I might have been interested," he allowed. "But I have a niece to raise now," he reminded her.

The man sounded a bit too noble, but who knew? For now, she didn't have any more time to wonder about him. Another story had come up on her schedule and needed her attention.

"I'll see you on Saturday," she told Colin pleasantly.

"See who on Saturday?" Jerry asked just as she hung up the phone on her desk.

She hadn't heard the cameraman come up behind her. "You need to get squeaky shoes," she told him. When he gave her a look that said he wasn't about to be distracted, she answered his question. "That detective we did the story on today."

"To finally tell him how you're connected?" Jerry

asked, curious. "Good for you. Did he call to tell you that he was having trouble placing you but that your name was sticking out for some reason?"

"No, he didn't," she said, trying not to get annoyed.

"Then why did he call?"

"He wants me to meet his niece."

Jerry dropped into the chair opposite her desk. Even sitting, he towered over her. "How's that again?" he asked, confused.

She gave him an instant replay. "The detective called, not very happy that we went ahead with the story without his okay—"

"The way you promised him," Jerry interjected, nodding his head.

"Yes, the way I promised him," she said between gritted teeth. And then she willed herself to calm down. Jerry meant well. There were just times that he didn't know how to go about it. "What did I do for a conscience before you came into my life?"

Jerry never hesitated. "My guess is that you were depraved and conniving."

Her eyes narrowed as she looked at him. "At least I didn't have to worry about someone eavesdropping on my conversations."

"Consider it a trade-off." He drew his chair in closer. "So how did you wind up saying you'd meet his niece?"

She smiled. "Seems his niece is a fan. At least, that's what it sounded like."

"So you're giving her a tour of the studio?" Colin asked.

From what she'd heard, the weekend promised to be rather hectic at the studio. Besides, this could be something she could save for a later date, like a virtual ace in the hole to be played when she felt she needed it.

Why was she making long-range plans about this man anyway? she silently asked herself. This was most likely going to be just a one-time thing. Done and over with. No reason to think otherwise.

She sounded like the typical distant celebrity as she said, "I thought it might be better just to do a little one-on-one. You know, answer her questions, give her an autographed photo, that kind of thing."

Jerry nodded. Crossing his arms before him, he gave her a penetrating look. "Any reason for the special treatment? Or do you feel that guilty about lying to our local hero?"

She frowned, enumerating it for her cameraman one more time. "A, I didn't lie. The station manager overruled me. B, I don't feel guilty about anything. And C, he isn't my local hero."

"Okay, then why are you doing this?" he asked.

"Maybe I'm just a nice person," she replied.

"Look, Ellie, I'm the first one in your corner—you know that. And yes, you're a nice person, but this is an extra mile here you're going. Maybe two. I'm just curious as to why."

He knew her too well, Ellie thought. Seeing no reason to keep this from him, she told him. "The girl lost both her parents six months ago. Maybe I feel like we're kindred spirits," Ellie said. "Anyway, he made it sound as if she was excited to meet me. I didn't see why I couldn't meet her. Satisfied?" she asked.

He gave her what his wife referred to as his "electric smile." It lit up his face and the immediate area. "Always."

"Uh-huh," she said dismissively, on her feet. "Let's get going. We've got another segment to film."

"I hear and obey," he told her as he followed her out.

For the rest of the week, the rendezvous she'd made with the detective over the phone to meet his niece was never far from Ellie's thoughts. It seemed to hover over her like a distant hummingbird that just wouldn't find a place to alight no matter how long it fluttered.

At least once a day, if not more, Ellie thought about calling and "regretfully" rescheduling. As the days until Saturday steadily disappeared, the idea of rescheduling grew more tempting.

In all honesty, Ellie had no idea what she was afraid of but her nerves were definitely on edge. It was somewhat akin to being aware that an earthquake was imminent and just waiting for the tremors to begin— without having a clue as to when they would hit.

It wasn't the prospect of meeting a ten-year-old that unsettled her. She got on fairly well with children, as well as with adults. But for some reason, it was the girl's uncle who had made her nervous.

Maybe she unconsciously blamed the detective, she theorized. Maybe, deep down in her soul, she felt he could have done something more and saved Brett. Or if he'd just arrived two minutes earlier, he could have prevented the robber from shooting Brett altogether.

No, she told herself fiercely, staring at her reflection in her bedroom mirror, she had to stop doing this to herself, had to stop coming up with what-ifs. Because it didn't matter "what if." What mattered was that it hadn't happened according to any one of the dozen scenarios she'd created. It had happened just one way and that way had resulted in Brett being the hero he always was and paying for that quality with his life.

To wonder about some other possible outcome was just going to make her crazy and she had to stop. Brett wouldn't have wanted her to continue to do this to herself. He would have wanted her to be happy. To live her life, she silently insisted.

So why was she looking into the mirror and crying? Ellie upbraided herself, angrily brushing the tears away with the back of her hand.

"Damn, now I've got to put my makeup on all over again," she complained. "You can't go meet this fan looking as if you've been peeling onions all morning," she told herself.

Taking a deep, steadying breath, Ellie went into her bathroom to wash her face and put on a fresh one. If she didn't hurry, she was going to be late.

"She's late," Heather observed, frowning, clearly worried about being stood up. They were sitting at a table in the café and it was fairly crowded, the way it was every Saturday at this time of day. Heather's eyes had been glued to the front door since they had arrived. She spared half a glance in her uncle's direction before her head whiplashed back into position. "Is your phone on?" she asked him.

"My phone's on," Colin assured his niece.

She put her hand out, still watching the front door. The hot chocolate in front of her was half-consumed and growing cold. "Can I see it?"

"Certainly not a trusting little girl, are you?" Colin quipped, shifting so he could get his cell phone out of his pocket.

"Trust but verify—you taught me that," Heather reminded him.

He laughed softly. "I didn't think you were listening." Rather than hand her the phone, Colin held it up in front of her so that she could see for herself. "Satisfied?"

She saw that it was active. "And you've got the ringer on?"

"Yes," he answered her patiently, "I've got the ringer on."

Heather frowned again. The door opened, but it was just a couple coming in. Heather sighed. "She said she'd call if she wasn't going to be here, right?"

"That's what the woman said. Heather," Colin said kindly, "she's probably just held up by traffic."

Instead of agreeing with him, Heather took the phone he still held in his hand and deftly pulled up the Sigalert app on it. Looking away from the door for a moment, she scanned the various routes.

"No traffic jams," she informed her uncle, handing the phone back to him.

"Then maybe she got a late start."

Colin looked at his niece. She was both old and young at the same time. An old soul trapped in a pre-teen's body and dealing with all those strange new feelings that were colliding with one another. Most likely, he was going to be in big trouble in about another year or two—if not sooner.

He supposed he should get Heather prepared just in case this didn't play out the way she hoped. "And even if she doesn't come, Heather, it's not like it's the end of the world."

Wide green eyes turned to him, clearly distressed. "I told my friends I was meeting her," she lamented.

Something didn't sound right. "Wait, I thought when I asked you just recently how things were going, you told me that you weren't making any friends." That had caused him some concern at the time.

Heather lifted her chin defensively. "Well, I made them."

"When?" he asked suspiciously.

"When I said you were bringing me to meet Elliana King," she told him, striking an innocent air.

"Heather, those aren't really friends," he said gently.

She was way ahead of him. "I know that, Uncle Colin. But I've got to start somewhere."

An old soul, he thought again as he rolled his eyes. "Sometimes I wonder who's raising who here."

"You're older, so you're the one raising me," she said matter-of-factly. Her heart-shaped face turned up to his, a hint of sadness welling up in her eyes as she made herself face the truth. "She's not coming, is she, Uncle Colin?"

"We don't know that yet." But if she didn't, he intended to go down to the news studio and make the woman realize how much she'd hurt his niece.

"But she's not," Heather insisted.

"Tell you what," he suggested. "Why don't I order you another hot chocolate? And when you finish drinking that, if that fancy news lady isn't here yet, we'll go home."

"And write her a nasty letter?"

"You bet," he agreed. "So nasty that the paper will burn her fingers when she holds it."

He was doing his best to hide his annoyance. The

woman had set the terms for this meeting and now she was disappointing Heather. It was one thing to go back on her word with him—he was thinking of the segment that had been aired—but quite another when it came to his niece. He took that as a personal affront and he promised himself that if Elliana King thought she'd heard the last of this, she had another think coming.

At the very least, she had—

"She's here!" Heather declared excitedly, rising in her seat and pointing toward the shop's entrance. Tugging urgently on his sleeve, she all but squealed, "She's here!"

Chapter Six

At first glance, Josie's Café seemed crowded, but then, Ellie already expected that. She'd had to park her car by the auto-parts store on the opposite side of the strip mall because there were no spots to be had by either the café or the round-the-clock fitness gym that was right next to it.

Saturday was the day that everyone was out catching up on their lives, mostly at the same time, Ellie thought wryly as she looked around the café, looking for Detective Benteen and his niece.

She was late and part of her wondered if maybe they had given up and left. She was late by only fifteen minutes, but she knew some people could be impatient and intolerant, easily feeling snubbed if strict punctuality wasn't adhered to. She'd actually thought of calling Benteen from her car to tell him she was on her way, but since she'd said she'd call only if she *wasn't* able to make the appointment, she'd been afraid he wouldn't answer and just take that as a signal to leave.

So Ellie now stood near the front entrance, scanning the small café and trying not to block other people's paths as they made their way in or out of the cozy family-owned establishment. The noise level was definitely up and that made focusing somewhat more difficult.

And then she saw them.

Oddly enough, it wasn't the young girl waving her arms and standing up by their table who caught Ellie's attention. Instead, she'd zeroed in on the detective who was seated next to the waving girl, his expression appearing somewhat grim.

Obviously, Ellie surmised, she'd incurred his disfavor by her late arrival. Well, that could be easily handled.

Waving back to the girl, Ellie quickly wound her way in and out of the pockets of space between people and tables as she forged a path to the table.

The first thing she did was to greet the girl rather than the detective she already knew.

"Hi! You must be Heather," Ellie said cheerfully, putting out her hand to the preteen.

Heather was at the age where she was testing the waters of being cool about things, but that role was abandoned for the time being as she eagerly put her hand into Ellie's and shook it with no small amount of enthusiasm.

"Yes, that's me. And you're really Elliana King," she cried.

"Last time I checked," Ellie answered with her

trademark warm, sunny smile. And then she added just a touch of contriteness to her voice as she said, "I'm sorry I'm late."

"Oh, we didn't notice," Heather told her loftily. "Did we, Uncle Colin?"

Colin had no idea why Heather was saying that, but he was wise enough to play along. This meeting was, after all, strictly for Heather's benefit.

"I don't own a watch," he said by way of backing up Heather's claim.

Colin saw amusement entering Ellie's eyes. He caught himself thinking that the woman had very expressive eyes. Beautiful expressive eyes.

Not that it mattered one way or another, he told himself as an afterthought.

"Even so, I am running late and I apologize. I hope you haven't been waiting long," Ellie said to the young girl.

As was her habit, she quickly took note of Heather's physical features, drawing a few conclusions. The preteen was willowy and taller than the average ten-year-old. That she was thin told Ellie that Heather didn't seek solace in food, which in turn told her that the girl either had extremely strong willpower or she was well adjusted with a good sense of self. Possibly both.

Heather instantly shook her head in response to Ellie's statement. "Oh no, we just got here ourselves."

Ellie glanced at the two cups on the table. Both more than half-empty.

"I guess they served you as you came in," Ellie said. "Must be good service here."

Rather than get flustered, Heather never missed a beat. "Oh, very good service," she attested.

Ellie smiled as she nodded, giving the girl another point for poise. Both Heather and her uncle were still on their feet. The latter had gotten up as she approached the table, which told Ellie that he'd been schooled in manners, something that wasn't all that common anymore.

"Well, let's sit down so we can get better acquainted," Ellie suggested.

Heather bobbed her head in agreement as she took her seat. Colin sat only after they did.

"Can I get you coffee?" Heather offered eagerly, bouncing up again.

Colin put his hand on his niece's shoulder and gently pushed her back into her seat. "I'll get Ms. King what she wants to drink so you two can talk," he said accommodatingly. Turning to the reporter, he asked, "What would you like?"

To ask you if you did everything you could that night.

The words popped into her head out of nowhere, startling her and making Ellie painfully aware that as much as she denied it, Jerry was right. She needed to tell the detective about their connection so it didn't hang over her head like this.

Soon, she promised herself.

Ellie forced a smile to her lips as she said, "Coffee, please."

"Decaf?" Colin asked. A lot of women he knew preferred the nonstimulating form of coffee.

But Ellie laughed at the question. "Not on your life. I need as much fuel as possible."

A woman after his own heart, he thought. "Cream and sugar?"

Ellie shook her head. "Black as midnight."

Heather looked pleased by the reporter's choice, Colin thought. "She likes her coffee the same way you do, Uncle Colin."

There was affection in his voice as he smiled at his niece. "Yes, I heard. Be right back," he promised a moment before he was all but swallowed up by the crowd he stepped into.

He'd said the words to his niece, not to her, Ellie noted, as if to reassure the girl he wasn't leaving her alone. Heather didn't strike her as being particularly insecure or nervous. Maybe it was habit, she guessed. In any event, she had to admit that she liked the man's protective attitude toward the girl. For someone who was new to this position of guardian, he seemed to be doing all right.

As if to confirm her thoughts, the next moment Heather said, "He's the best."

Ellie nodded, absently acknowledging the girl's testimony.

And then Heather seemed to roll the statement over in her mind again. "Well, maybe a little more than he used to be."

"How so?" Ellie asked. Even if the woman in her had more or less retreated from the human race, the reporter in Ellie was curious about everything.

Heather seemed to choose her words carefully before answering. "He's just getting the hang of being a dad instead of an uncle."

That told her that he'd been a presence in the girl's life even before her parents had died. It spoke well of the man. Usually someone Benteen's age didn't have time for girls unless they were over the age of eighteen.

"So he's different now?" she asked Heather.

Heather nodded. "A little. He checks my homework and does a bunch of other stuff he didn't do when he was just my uncle."

"And how do you feel about that?" Ellie asked.

Heather appeared to consider her answer before giving it.

"Okay, I guess." And then a lightbulb went off over her head. "Hey, are you interviewing me?" the girl asked.

Ellie was nothing if not warm as she gave her answer. "Well, I'm getting to know you and that's the way I get to know people, so yes, I guess in a way I am interviewing you. Do you mind?" she asked.

"No, it's cool."

Ellie smiled. "And so are you," she told Heather. The girl beamed in response, obviously thrilled by the compliment. "Would you like to be a reporter someday?"

Heather paused to seriously think the question over. "I'm not sure yet. First I want to graduate the fourth grade."

Ellie bit the inside of her bottom lip to keep from laughing. She didn't want to hurt the girl's feelings. "I see you have your priorities straight."

The next moment, Colin rejoined them at the table. "Here we go," he said, "Coffee, black as midnight, just as you requested." He placed the cup in front of Ellie and then took his seat. He noticed that Heather was practically beaming. "So, what are you two talking about?"

"Graduating fourth grade," Ellie answered him. Humor entered her eyes as she looked back at his niece. "And having your priorities straight."

Colin picked up his own cup and pretended to toast them, then took a sip. "Okay, I guess I'm all caught up, then," he commented.

"Would you like to ask me any questions?" Ellie asked, looking at Heather.

Heather looked as if she was fairly bursting to ask questions. The only problem was which to ask first and which to leave for a later time. "Do you ever get nervous?"

"You mean on the air?" Ellie asked. She smiled in response. "Sure, lots of times."

"Really?" It wasn't that Heather didn't believe her; she looked as if she was thrilled to discover that her newest idol was human.

"Really," Ellie repeated.

"But you never look nervous."

Ellie leaned in confidentially toward the girl. "Want to know a little trick?"

"Sure!" Heather answered enthusiastically.

Ellie told her the truth. "That's because I pretend it's just the person and me, talking as if we were old friends."

"Like we're talking now?" Heather asked as she realized that was exactly what was happening. Ellie was talking to her as if they had always known each other.

"Like we're talking now," Ellie confirmed.

The woman was good with Heather, Colin thought, and he appreciated it. Because she was, he didn't want to abuse Ellie's time or her patience.

"If you have anything else you want to ask Ms.

King, why don't you do it now?" Colin urged his niece. "I'm sure that Ms. King is very busy and we don't want to keep her from her work."

Ellie looked at him, masking her surprise. He was actually using the excuse she had prepared to use. But now that she was here, she found that despite her reservations—and that one rather dark cloud that was hanging between them—she wanted to stay awhile. She was enjoying Heather's company. The girl was both older than her years and yet still refreshingly untarnished and innocent. That was rare these days when ten-year-olds were going on twenty in ways that would take innocence away from them.

"Actually, I cleared this morning so I could do this," she told Heather, throwing the detective a quick glance, as well. "So go for it," she encouraged. "Ask away."

Heather grinned like a child who had just been admitted to Santa's workshop in late November. All the newly built toys had yet to be wrapped up and accounted for—so she could have her pick.

"Okay."

They'd been talking for more than an hour. For the most part, it had been Heather asking questions and Ellie answering them. Occasionally, Colin would slip in a question himself. He had to admit that he was surprised that the news reporter turned out to be so accessible and human.

He hadn't known exactly what to expect when he'd initially set up this meeting. He supposed he'd expected a plastic would-be celebrity, someone playing the part of a so-called reporter/personality until she grew tired of answering questions or pretending to answer questions. But Ellie King wasn't plastic. Unlike some of her counterparts, she seemed to be *very* genuine. He appreciated the fact that she was interacting with his niece and treating her not like an underling or a child but like a person who mattered.

As for Heather, he could see that she was really enjoying this. It did his heart good to see her like this. It was the first time he'd seen the old Heather, the girl she'd been before her life had been so cruelly stripped of both her parents. Before she was made to face the fact that life had a very real dark underbelly.

He realized that he had the reporter to thank for that, at least in part. By paying attention to Heather, by treating her like a person whose feelings were important, the woman had allowed this side of Heather to resurface.

He was about to say something to Ellie to get her to understand that he was grateful for this when his cell phone began to ring, interrupting his train of thought. Colin frowned even before he checked the screen to see who was calling.

Part of him already knew.

Wound up like a top, Heather abruptly stopped talking and glanced at her uncle as he took out his phone and swiped the screen to take the call.

Ellie saw the look on the girl's face. "Something wrong?" she asked Heather.

"It's probably work," Heather said in a subdued voice, suppressing a sigh.

"I've got to take this," Colin told her. With that, he left the table.

"Does this happen a lot?" Ellie asked the girl, trying to sound sympathetic at the same time.

"It happens enough times," Heather confirmed. She shrugged philosophically, trying to make it seem as if it didn't bother her. "They need him."

"I'm sure they do," Ellie told her, putting her hand over the girl's.

Heather smiled her gratitude.

The call was short. They always were. Pocketing his phone, Colin came back to the table. He didn't sit down. By the look on Heather's face, he knew that she already knew what he was going to say. For once he really wished he didn't have to, but there was no way around it.

"Sorry, honey. We're going to have to end this. I've got to get you home and get Olga to come to stay with you."

"Olga's the Russian lady next door," Heather explained to Ellie before turning her emotive eyes up to her uncle. "Do you have to go?" she asked.

"I'm sorry, Heather, but I'm afraid so." He turned toward the reporter. "Thank you for meeting us like this. It was really very nice of you—"

Ellie cut him off before he could finish. "There's no need for it to end."

"I'm afraid there is. I've got to get Heather home," Colin began to explain again in case the woman didn't get it.

Ellie held her hand up, stopping him again. "Why don't I follow you and stay with Heather while you're gone?" She flashed a smile at Heather. "We girls can just keep on talking."

For a second, Colin was speechless, fully aware that

Heather was pleading with him with her eyes, asking him to agree. In good conscience, he knew he couldn't.

"I don't know how long I'll be gone," he told the woman.

He couldn't expect her to hang around until he came home. Olga, on the other hand, was accustomed to popping over and remaining until all hours. Besides, he paid the woman for her time. She'd initially protested, but they'd worked out equitable rates. Fortunately, her work time at the cleaning service was flexible enough for her to be able to make these arrangements.

Ellie, however, seemed determined. She must have seen how much Heather wanted to go on talking with her.

"I fully understand," she told the detective. "Tell you what. Why don't you give me this Olga's number and if I have to leave for some reason before you can get back, I'll call her to come over?"

At that point, Heather stopped pleading with her eyes and her mouth took over, as did her hands, which she used to clutch his arm, as if that would somehow give her more leverage.

"Please, Uncle Colin? Say yes."

He in turn looked at the reporter making what he considered to be a rather generous offer. "You sure about this?"

"I said I cleared my morning—and to be honest, I cleared the rest of my day, as well. I was going to go shopping," she confided. "But this is a lot more satisfying than going shopping. Apparently, I underestimated the number of questions Heather would have for me." Her eyes met Heather's and she winked at the girl. "Seems like we just started to scratch the surface."

Heather mouthed "Thank you" to her, then turned back toward her uncle.

"Please?" Heather begged again.

Colin sighed. "If I say no, I'm an ogre," he commented.

"And we really can't have that," Ellie told him even as she appeared to agree with his conclusion. "Nobody likes an ogre."

He'd always had trouble saying no to Heather, although now that he'd become both mother and father to her, there were instances when he had to. But this didn't really need to be one of them. And as long as the reporter didn't seem to mind, who was he to say no?

"All right, as long as you're all right with this, I'm not the one who's going to kill this little get-together," Colin said.

Heather was all but bouncing up and down in her seat. "Oh, thank you!" she cried excitedly.

"Okay, then, where are you parked?" he asked Ellie, getting down to logistics.

"In the north forty," she quipped, standing up. "Why don't you give me a few minutes to pull up in front of the café so that I can follow your car? Better yet, give me your address in case I lose sight of the car."

Before he could try one more time to demur, Heather was rattling off their address. Ellie quickly wrote it down on her napkin and put it into her purse.

"Got it," she announced.

You certainly do, Colin couldn't help thinking, feeling as if he'd gotten swept off his feet by a hurricane.

And with that, it was a done deal.

Chapter Seven

Colin was completely and utterly exhausted as he unlocked his front door.

For a while there, it looked as if he wasn't going to be able to come home at all tonight. But then he caught a break and just like that, the case was put to rest. At least as far as he was concerned.

They'd been shorthanded at the station, so when the call went out regarding an Amber Alert, his was the next name on the backup rotation and he'd been called down. But it had ended well, which ultimately was all that really mattered.

Colin finally let himself into his apartment. Not for the first time he thought, *Thank God for Olga.* Otherwise he would have been really hard-pressed to get someone to stay with Heather at a moment's notice the way his job at times necessitated.

As he closed the door behind him, Colin heard the TV. He recognized some of the dialogue. A series marathon was running on one of the cable channels. Olga favored that program, telling him she watched it in order to try to perfect her English. He suspected the fact that the leading man was exceptionally good-looking might have had something to do with it, as well.

Walking into the living room, he was about to greet his neighbor but then stopped dead in his tracks. Instead of the pleasantly rounded grandmotherly woman who periodically brought over baked goods and "leftovers" that suspiciously didn't look as if they were leftovers at all, he was looking at Ellie King sitting on his recliner.

"You're not Olga."

Ellie'd been dozing off and on during the last hour but was now instantly awake. She sat up, her eyes meeting his.

"I don't know if that's an observation or an accusation," she responded, the corners of her mouth curving.

Glancing past the woman, Colin saw that his niece was on the sofa, curled up like a kitten and very soundly asleep.

"What happened?" Colin asked.

Ellie's brain still felt slightly foggy. She rose from the recliner, pulling herself together. "What do you mean?"

Colin rephrased his question. "Why didn't you go home?"

"We didn't finish talking. Your niece *really* likes to talk," she told him with a laugh.

"And you stayed?" he asked, surprised. Colin noticed that Heather was covered with a throw that he kept on the back of the sofa. This had to be the reporter's work.

"Well, it seemed kind of rude to walk out on Heather in midsentence. Besides, I was enjoying her company." She glanced at the girl and smiled. "And I kind of think she was enjoying mine."

In his mind, there was no doubt. "Oh, I'm sure she was. She couldn't wait for Saturday to come so she could meet you. But once she fell asleep, why didn't you call Olga to come over?" he asked. "Don't you have somewhere else you have to be?"

It was one o'clock in the morning. The only place she had to be at that time of night was in bed.

Ellie shrugged, dismissing his question. "If I did, Detective, I assure you I'd be there. No, this turned out to be one of those rare days where I was the mistress of my own fate, able to spend my day doing anything I wanted to."

"So you chose to spend it with a ten-year-old?" he asked incredulously. That didn't sound very plausible to him. Ellie was considered a celebrity of sorts. Celebrities didn't choose to hang out with ten-year-olds unless they were related to them.

"A very precocious, entertaining ten-year-old," Ellie amended. There was a fond expression on her face as she looked at the sleeping girl again. "She's really a great kid," she told him.

"I know," he responded, looking at his niece. "That's why I worry about her." He wanted to protect her, to keep Heather from getting hurt. But there was no way to Bubble Wrap her world—or even her.

"You shouldn't," Ellie told him. "In my humble

opinion, Heather's amazingly well adjusted and bright, and I have a feeling she'll go far." Her eyes shifted back to the detective. "And she speaks very highly of you, you know."

"You talked about me?" Colin asked her, clearly surprised.

"*She* talked about you," Ellie clarified, not wanting him to get the wrong idea. "I just listened. In her estimation, you're about ten feet tall and stop just short of leaping over tall buildings in a single bound," she said, amused.

Because Heather was asleep in the living room and he didn't want to wake her just yet, Colin indicated that they should move into the kitchen. He pulled out a chair at the table and sat down.

Debating her exit, Ellie decided to join him for just a minute. "There's some dinner, if you're interested," she told him. When he looked at her curiously, she pointed to a covered pan on the stove.

"Olga stopped by?" he asked. If she had, why hadn't the woman stayed?

The next moment, Ellie answered the question for him. "No, I made it."

"You cook?"

Someone else might have taken offense at his obvious stereotypical view of her, but Ellie let it go, choosing instead to just be amused.

"I can do more than hold a microphone in my hand, yes," she said, addressing a more elaborate question that she assumed was going through his mind. "Nothing fancy, just some fried chicken breasts," she told him, adding, "They're still warm, if you're hungry."

The moment she said the word, he realized that he

actually was. Very hungry. With good reason. "Other than the coffee this morning, all I've had is some stale pizza left over in the break room, so fried chicken sounds pretty good to me, warm or cold."

She was already uncovering the pan and taking out a piece of chicken to put on a plate.

"Then by all means, eat," she urged, placing the plate in front of him. Without thinking, she took a seat opposite him. "Did you get your bad guy?"

For just a moment, Colin lost himself in the taste of the chicken cutlet he'd bitten into. It wasn't just good; it was *very* good. He relished it, then realized that the woman had asked him something. The words, however, were lost to him.

So he looked up at her, puzzled. "What?"

Ellie began to explain. "I assumed that whatever called you away involved a bad guy of some sort. I was just wondering if you got him."

She flashed a smile at him, knowing that she was invading territory he might not be at liberty to talk about yet. In her experience, police personnel had this maddening habit of asking questions but not answering them when they were involved in an ongoing case. It always made her want to dig deeper.

When the detective didn't say anything in reply, she assumed that this was another one of those "no comment" instances. Ellie began to get up from the table. "You don't have to tell me," she said, resigned.

He was eating—and really enjoying—the chicken she'd made. His mouth was full of the savory flavor, which was why he couldn't answer her. In lieu of that, he made a noise and waved her back down in her seat.

"You want me to sit. Okay." She complied, sinking back down in the chair for the moment. She noted how he was doing away with the piece of chicken she'd served him. Some would call it doing it justice, she thought, rather pleased.

"Is this because you want me to stick around until you're sure I didn't poison you?" she deadpanned.

"You don't look like you'd poison anyone," Colin told her when he could finally speak.

"Ever see a picture of Lucrezia Borgia?" Ellie posed innocently.

Colin shook his head before taking another forkful of the crisp chicken meat. "You do like to keep people guessing, don't you?"

"That's what makes life exciting," Ellie replied. "Well, since you're still obviously alive," she began philosophically, getting up again, "I'll consider dinner a success and let myself out."

She was about to walk out when she heard Colin say, "We got him."

Turning around to look at the detective, Ellie asked, "Excuse me?"

"You asked if we got the bad guy," he reminded her. "We did."

She smiled, pleased that he'd answered her but now exceedingly curious about the details that went with the story.

"Congratulations," she told him, doubling back to rejoin him.

"He wasn't actually a bad guy," Colin said, amending his previous statement. "Maybe a more accurate description of him is that he wasn't a bad person—he was just very frustrated."

Reclaiming her chair, Ellie sat down for a third

time. He'd phrased it that way on purpose, she thought, to lure her back in. That in itself surprised her. She would have thought he'd be happy to see her go.

How about you? Why aren't you making good your exit? Why are you hanging around the man who couldn't save your husband?

She didn't have a good answer to that.

Instead, she heard herself telling him, "You know I'm not going to let it go at just that, don't you?" The expression on his face told her that he knew. But he was eating again and his mouth was full. "I can wait," she said, leaning back in the chair.

"It was an abduction," he revealed once his mouth was empty and he could speak again.

That got Ellie's attention and she slid to the edge of her seat. "He kidnapped somebody? Who?" This time when Colin brought the fork up to his lips again, she caught his arm, stopped him. "Who?" she repeated.

"His daughter." Colin shook his head. Both parties were to blame in this. "It was a custody battle gone really wrong. Father got tired of being stonewalled, so when it came time for him to bring his five-year-old daughter back after a scheduled visit, he didn't. The mother had a meltdown and called us."

"And you found him?" Ellie asked, clearly impressed. She made no effort to hide the fact.

He didn't want to make it sound as if he was the hero of the piece. It was luck more than anything else. "There was an Amber Alert out. Someone called in saying they'd spotted the father's car going south on the 5 Freeway. We wound up cornering the guy twenty miles outside of San Diego."

"You?" she asked specifically.

"And the other detective in the car," he added. "It was a team effort."

She knew how these things worked. What she was surprised at was that Benteen was being so modest. The man really didn't like being in the spotlight. "How's the little girl?" she asked.

"Scared." The scene played in his mind again. It had been difficult to witness and even more difficult to do "the right thing."

"She didn't want to leave her father. Seems she wanted to be with him instead of her mother."

"Little girls do love their daddies," Ellie commented. However, that wasn't always the case, which caused her to ask, "Did she say why?"

Colin recalled the little girl's words. "'Daddy's more fun.' She said her mother had too many rules she had to follow."

"Rules can be good," Ellie interjected, thinking of what Heather had said about her uncle having been more fun before she'd become his responsibility. She couldn't help wondering if the girl had ever said that to the detective. That could have been the reason he seemed so sensitive retelling the tale.

"Yeah, but a kid needs fun," Colin countered. He frowned slightly, thinking of the man they had taken into custody. "Hated having to take the guy in. All he wanted was to be with his daughter." He sighed. "I told him that he and his wife should have found a way to work it out for the little girl's sake—and that he could still try."

"In a perfect world…"

Her voice trailed off, but Colin knew what she was

saying. In a perfect world, there would be happy endings no matter how rocky the road to get there might be.

If only...

"But this isn't a perfect world," Colin said, more to himself that to her.

A shaft of sadness speared through her, making her heart ache. Tears came into her eyes even though she tried to block them. Sometimes all it took was a word, a familiar scent, a lyric, and she was catapulted into the past, reliving it again. Always with the same ending.

"No," she whispered, "It's not a perfect world."

For a second, Colin thought that the woman had been affected by the story he'd just told her. If that was the case, the reporter had an incredible sense of empathy, he felt, amazed.

And then, literally out of nowhere, a fragment of a thought darted through his mind, bringing with it a flash of the last case he'd had as a patrolman. He was on his knees in a convenience store, desperately trying to stop a man's life from oozing away.

Why the hell had he thought of that now? Colin upbraided himself. What possible connection did it have with the case he'd had tonight?

And then he realized it *wasn't* the Amber Alert case that had made him think of the other one; it was the name. The reporter's last name.

King.

He looked at the woman now, then dismissed it. It couldn't be. King was a pretty common surname. If there had been a connection between her and the man who had died on the floor of that store that night, the reporter would have said something.

Wouldn't she?

Sure she would. Talking was what she did. She would have brought it up by now.

He was just tired, Colin told himself. More than tired, he was wiped out.

"Something wrong?" she asked him, approaching the subject cautiously, like someone tasked with defusing a bomb.

"No," he said, then explained, "Just something I thought of. But it doesn't make sense." Colin shrugged, dismissing the stray thought. "It's nothing, just my overworked mind."

That was her cue to leave. More like escape, Ellie silently corrected. In either case, the man needed his sleep. So did she, although she didn't sleep all that well anymore.

"And I'm keeping you up, so I'm going to leave now," Ellie told him, getting up.

"You also fed me," he said, indicating the empty plate. "And I have to say that was really good."

She took the plate and deposited it into his sink. "Well, you don't 'have to,' but I'll take it as a compliment."

He rose to his feet because she had. "Do you do this kind of thing often?" he asked.

She turned to look at him, bemused. "What? Take compliments?"

"No." He nodded toward his sleeping niece. "Go out of your way like this to spend time with a fan."

Ellie smiled as she shrugged. "Why not? It's good for my ego."

She didn't strike him as someone with an ego. He also noticed she didn't answer the question. He let it go. "I know that you made her day. Heather really appreciated this—so do I."

She picked up her messenger bag and secured it across her shoulder. "Call it payback."

Colin wasn't following her. "For what?"

That had just slipped out and she hadn't meant it to. Her mind scrambled to do a little damage control, searching for an explanation she could give him.

"For the interview segment I did on you earlier this week," she finally said.

"Oh, that." He waved it away as he walked her the short distance to the front door. "To be honest, I really didn't think I was going to get to review the footage before you aired it."

She didn't understand. "Then why did you call to tell me I lied?"

"Probably to teach you not to make promises you couldn't deliver—and I thought it might be a way to get you to agree to meet Heather," he admitted. "I was just hoping you'd give her an autograph or something." He glanced back into the living room, where his niece was sleeping. "This is something she's going to remember for a long, long time," he told the reporter.

Ellie put his words into a more realistic setting. "Until she gets her first crush on a boy and he's nice to her."

Colin groaned. "Boys. Oh God, I hope that doesn't happen for another ten years or so."

"Good luck with that," Ellie laughed. "Your niece is very advanced for her age," she pointed out. "Try another six months—or less."

He almost seemed to go pale right in front of her eyes. "You're kidding, right?"

"Do you even remember girls at that age?" she prodded. "Think back to when you were ten or eleven."

"I was a saint," he told her. He almost managed to say the words with a straight face.

"I really doubt that." Ellie gave him a highly skeptical look.

"What makes you say that?" he asked, doing his best not to smirk precisely because he *did* recall himself at that age.

"Let's just call it keen reporter's instincts," she told him, patting his face. "Good night, Detective," Ellie said as she crossed the threshold onto his doorstep. "It's been an interesting evening in more ways than one."

"Same here," he told her.

Colin stood in his doorway, watching as the woman walked to her car in guest parking. He continued standing there as she got in behind the steering wheel.

"Good night, Ellie King," he murmured.

As he closed his door, Colin couldn't shake the feeling that he was missing something.

Chapter Eight

The deliveryman threaded his way across various cables and wires that were on the studio floor, not an easy feat, given that his vision was partially blocked by the large profusion of flowers he was carrying and charged with delivering. Whenever possible, he stopped to ask where he could find the intended recipient of the flowers.

The last person he asked pointed him to Ellie's desk. But when he set down the arrangement, there was no one sitting at the desk.

Haplessly, the deliveryman looked around for someone he could snag long enough to have them put their signature on the electronic pad he'd tucked under his arm.

"Um, I need to have someone sign for this," he said, raising his voice and hoping to get someone's attention.

Hearing what almost amounted to a plea as he entered the bull pen, Jerry quickly cut across the floor to Ellie's desk in order to put the man out of his misery.

"Here, I'll sign," Jerry volunteered. With a flourish, Jerry signed his name with the stylus that was attached to the pad. Giving the pad back to the deliveryman, he glanced at the effusive basket and commented, "Nice arrangement."

"Boss insists on the best," the deliveryman replied, glancing over the pad to make sure everything was in order. An automatic smile momentarily came over his lips as he said, "Have a good day."

"Yeah, you, too," Jerry murmured. Because he had signed for the delivery, he felt that gave him the right to peek at the card, which he did. And then he smiled. "Well, well, well."

"'Well' what?" Ellie asked, entering the room from the opposite direction. She'd just finished reviewing several upcoming segments with the program manager, including the one he wanted taped today. The clock was ticking.

Jerry stepped back, giving her a clear view of her desk. He gestured grandly toward the basket. "Well, it looks like someone made a good impression on someone else."

Seeing the flowers for the first time, Ellie stopped walking. No one sent her flowers. Her first thought was that it had to be a mistake. The flowers were meant for someone else.

She looked at Jerry. "Where did those come from?"

"My guess is it wasn't the flower fairy." He grinned, unable to contain himself. He parked himself on the edge of her desk, leaning his hip against it. "So, you talked with the detective like I suggested."

Her eyes widened. "These are from him?" she asked, quickly crossing the rest of the distance to her desk.

"See for yourself. There's the card." Jerry pointed to it. Cocking his head to underscore the innocent tone he affected, he asked, "Who's Heather?"

"Detective Benteen's niece," Ellie answered, searching through the flowers for the card. "You ask more questions than my mother." Finding the card, she pulled it out. "What are you doing reading my card, anyway?"

"Someone had to sign for the flowers," he told her. "I figured that entitled me to see who sent them." Since she hadn't acknowledged what he'd said earlier, he repeated himself. "I guess you and the good detective had that talk and came to terms, eh?"

Ellie refused to answer him. Instead, she read the card. *Thank you for Saturday. I haven't seen Heather this happy in a long, long time.*

Ellie looked up to see Jerry watching her smugly. She knew it would have been a lot easier just to let her cameraman assume that he was right, but she wasn't in the habit of lying, even about minor things, and she didn't want Jerry thinking she'd followed his advice when she hadn't yet. The man had a big enough ego as it was.

"If you must know, no," she said, annoyed. "We didn't have that talk. He asked me to meet his niece. Turns out that she's a fan, so I said sure. We met at Josie's Café. It was only supposed to be for an hour, but while we were talking, he got a call telling him to come to the scene of a crime. I volunteered to stay with his niece until he got back."

It was more complicated than that, but there was no point in going into babysitting neighbors or any of the rest of what had been involved. She was trying to keep her story streamlined.

Ellie glanced at Jerry and saw the knowing expression on her cameraman's face. It was bordering on a smirk.

"Don't give me that look," she told him.

"What look?" he asked innocently.

"You're grinning," Ellie accused.

"Who, me?" he said with far too much feeling. "No. I'm just enjoying listening to you tell your story." And then he gave up the ruse. "It's just nice to see you getting out again."

"I wasn't 'getting out,'" she insisted, knowing that the cameraman thought she'd gone out with the detective. It wasn't like that. "I was just—" Ellie gave up. There was no point in beating her head against the wall. Jerry was going to see things his way no matter what she said to the contrary. "Oh, never mind. Marty wants us to cover a story at Bedford's animal shelter. Grab your gear," she ordered.

"Animal shelter?" Jerry repeated as he hurried after her. "Are you sure?"

"Yes, why?" She spared him a look over her shoulder. To her relief, the flowers—and the reason for them—had been forgotten.

For now.

"Last time we did one of those stories, I came home with a geriatric dog and a rabbit. Betsy wasn't very happy about it," he recalled. "If I come home with any-

thing else, she's going to put us all out on the drive-
way."

Ellie laughed because she knew Jerry's distress was
genuine. He might talk big, but he had a heart made
out of mush.

"Just stay strong, Jerry—and remember to say no,"
she advised.

"I can't help it if I have a marshmallow center," he
protested, hustling behind her.

"It goes well with your marshmallow build," Ellie
deadpanned.

Jerry grumbled under his breath. Ellie pretended not
to hear him. At least he wasn't asking any more questions about her meeting with the detective, she thought,
relieved. She had a hard enough time trying to figure
out why she'd done it herself, much less answering any
of the questions Jerry could come up with.

The next moment, she put the whole thing out of
her mind. She had a segment to tape and it deserved
her full attention.

The assignment ran twice as long as she'd anticipated.

The shelter, it turned out, was also planning to have
an adopt-a-pet event that following Saturday and the
people in charge were using the volunteer drive she
had been sent to cover to promote that.

Ellie had always had a weak spot for animals.
Caught up in the story, Ellie found herself losing her
heart to a mixed-breed puppy with the improbable
name of Pancakes. Pancakes was all paws, licking
tongue and tons of unbridled energy.

Before she realized it, Ellie had paid the very nominal fee the shelter charged for the dog's shots, a certificate of ownership and a license. And just like that, she became Pancakes's new owner.

"I can't keep you, you know," Ellie informed the puppy, who was riding in the back of her sedan. Not exactly riding, she amended. Pancakes was running back and forth on the floor like a claustrophobic prison inmate searching for an avenue of escape. "I sprung you in a moment of weakness because you are just the cutest thing I've ever seen, but it wouldn't be fair to you if I took you home. I'm hardly ever there. You need a hands-on owner." Coming to a stop at a red light, she glanced over her shoulder to her frantic furry passenger. "You realize that, don't you?"

Ellie sighed. "Lord, I must be losing it—I'm having a conversation with a dog. A one-way conversation." At which point the dog yipped. "Okay, maybe not so one-way," she corrected herself, putting her foot back on the accelerator. "But you still need someone who can walk you and play with you. I'm hardly home long enough to put my laundry away."

Pancakes yipped again, louder this time.

"You need a keeper, you know." And then she thought of the flowers on her desk.

Belatedly, she remembered that she hadn't had a chance to call Benteen to thank him yet. This would be a way to thank him and to get Pancakes a home that was more suited to his energetic personality.

Ellie smiled. Two birds with one stone.

Perfect!

"Hang on, Pancakes—I'm going to take you to your new home."

Ellie made a sharp right at the next corner.

* * *

Fifteen minutes later, overzealous puppy in her arms and carrying a bag of dry dog food she'd bought at the shelter, Ellie found herself standing in front of Colin Benteen's door. She knocked once and mentally crossed her fingers that he was home.

Colin had gotten home in time to watch the evening broadcast of the news with Heather. She talked through most of it until the segment with Ellie came on. Then his niece became as silent as a tomb, rabidly watching every move her idol made and listening to every word as if each one of them was a singular golden pearl of wisdom. The fact that Ellie's segment tonight was filmed in the city's animal shelter, with Ellie surrounded by a dozen yapping dogs and one duck that seemed to think it too was a dog, only endeared her all the more to Heather.

The segment and Heather's reaction to it were still very fresh in his mind as Colin went to answer the door. He hadn't heard from Ellie and was beginning to wonder if perhaps he'd overstepped his bounds by sending her flowers.

Had he offended her? Or maybe she felt that he was crowding her. Since she hadn't called, he could only assume that it was one or the other, or possibly a combination of both.

Then he opened his door and all his theories and suppositions were immediately placed on hold. It was as if she had materialized out of his thoughts and onto his doorstep. What really captivated his attention was what she appeared to be holding in her arms.

At first it just looked like a mass of moving light tan fur mixed with shafts of white. But the very next moment it barked and the mystery of what she was holding was solved.

Like an international call to attention, the bark also managed to instantly draw Heather to the door. The next moment, she was grinning from ear to ear.

"Ellie, you're here!" she exclaimed excitedly.

"Bearing fur," Colin observed wryly.

"Actually," Ellie said, doing her best to hold on to Pancakes, who was doing *her* very best *not* to be held on to, "I came to bring Heather a present."

Heather's eyes suddenly widened to the point that they looked as if they were in danger of falling out. "That's for me?" she cried, immediately assuming that her new best friend was referring to the dog that was just barely contained in her arms.

Ellie turned toward Colin, who was still holding the door open like a conscientious sentry. "May I come in?" she asked him.

"Sorry." Realizing that he was standing there rigidly, Colin stepped back and opened his front door farther. "You took me by surprise," he admitted by way of an excuse.

"This was all very spur-of-the-moment," Ellie said, indicating the puppy she'd brought over. "I was shooting a segment at the local pet shelter today and this puppy—"

Heather cut in. "We just saw it!" She pointed toward the TV monitor as if it would bear her out. "The duck was funny."

"The duck has serious issues," Ellie cracked.

Heather's eyes never left the puppy that was frantically searching for a way to jump down, twisting and turning like an escape artist in a straitjacket. Not standing on ceremony, Heather began to pet the puppy's head and was rewarded with a tongue bath on her hand. Heather giggled.

"Is this the puppy you were holding on the show?" she asked eagerly.

"The puppy I was *trying* to hold on the show," Ellie corrected.

"Did they give him to you?" Heather asked.

Ellie laughed. Out of the corner of her eye, she saw the smile that came to the detective's lips. She wasn't sure if he was laughing at her or at the situation. For now she left it unexplored.

"It's a her," she corrected. "And it was more like she just refused to let me leave once we stopped rolling."

"I guess it looks like you have a puppy, then," Colin concluded as he joined his niece in petting the hyper animal.

"What's her name?" Heather asked.

"Pancakes," Ellie told her. "Don't look at me," she told Colin. "I had nothing to do with it. That's the name she came with."

"And she's yours?" Heather asked, still stroking the puppy.

"Well, I paid her fees," Ellie said, transferring the puppy from her arms to Heather's. "But she's not exactly mine," she continued. When both Heather and her uncle looked at her for an explanation, Ellie told them, "I'm not home long enough to give this dog the proper attention." She kept her gaze on Heather, deliberately avoiding making eye contact with Colin for the time being. "I thought that maybe you'd like to have a pet."

Heather looked so happy that for a second she

looked as if she was about to burst. "You're giving Pancakes to me?" she cried, barely able to contain her joy.

Ellie glanced toward the detective. She knew this was a roundabout and underhanded way of doing this, but she was rather desperate. "If it's okay with your uncle," she qualified.

Heather instantly turned her expressive green eyes on her uncle. "Please, Uncle Colin?" the girl pleaded. "Please?"

As if to reinforce her new would-be owner's pleas, the puppy began to madly lick Colin's face.

Laughing, Colin held the dog at arm's length before telling his niece, "You're going to be the one responsible for this bundle of fur."

"Absolutely!" Heather vowed.

Colin wasn't finished. "You'll have to walk her, feed her, make sure she stays off the furniture—and doesn't chew the furniture," he emphasized, pulling the puppy away from the corner of the sofa that Pancakes had begun to attack. The puppy was clearly teething.

"Yes, yes, yes," Heather answered each question with enthusiasm. She scooped the puppy back up into her arms, giggling as she felt her neck being licked. "So I can keep her?"

"For now," Colin warned. "But if you fall down on the job, if you start forgetting to feed her, to play with her, she's going to have to go back."

"To the shelter?" Heather cried, obviously stunned that her uncle could be that strict, even though it was a known fact, one that Ellie had emphasized in her story, that the shelter had a no-kill policy no matter how crowded it became.

"No, to the news reporter who brought her," Colin told her, glancing at Ellie.

Ellie put her arm around the girl's shoulders, giving her a light squeeze. "I'm sure that she'll do an excellent job, won't you, Heather?" she asked, looking down at the preteen.

"I will, oh, I will," Heather promised keenly.

"If you're interested," Ellie told both Colin and his niece, "Pancakes has had all her shots." She opened her messenger bag and took out several sheets of paper documenting the puppy's care and the shots she'd received. "Here's her health history and her license. She's all paid up for a year."

Colin took the papers from her and placed them on the counter. "And you're not keeping her because—?"

"I don't have enough time to properly take care of her." She looked at the bundle of love on four paws. "It's a shame and I wish I did, but it just wouldn't be fair to Pancakes to keep her locked up all day when I'm away, working."

Still holding the puppy in her arms, Heather was being rewarded with a bath of what she referred to as "doggy kisses." She looked, Colin noted, as if she'd died and gone to heaven.

"You can come visit her anytime you want," she told Ellie.

She appreciated the invitation, but there was something else to consider. "I think that might be up to your uncle, honey."

Both Heather and Ellie stared in his direction.

On the spot, Colin saw no reason to put up any obstacles. When he came right down to it, he welcomed an excuse to see the sexy reporter more often. She was really beginning to intrigue him—and it was obvious that Heather idolized her. She'd managed to get to his niece the way he hadn't been able to in six months.

"Sure, why not?" he said.

"Okay," Ellie said, nodding, "I'll take you up on that sometime." About to leave, she suddenly remembered what had been behind this visit in the very first place. "Oh, by the way, I almost forgot. I loved the flowers."

"So you did get them. Good."

She felt she owed him an explanation as to why she'd been so remiss expressing her thanks. "They arrived just as I had to go do the animal-shelter story, so I didn't have an opportunity to call you. You didn't have to send them," she added.

"And you didn't have to stay as long as you did Saturday, or prepare dinner," he told her.

Ellie nodded. "I guess then we're even."

He glanced at the puppy that seemed to be all teeth and paws as she climbed up Heather's arm. The puppy was like the very personification of trouble.

"Oh, I don't know about that," Colin speculated, then laughed. "I think the balance might be just a little off in this case."

Ellie inclined her head, unaware that her smile had managed to captivate the detective. "Maybe you're right. I'll pay for any initial damages," she offered.

He nodded. "That would be a start." And then he changed the subject. "Have you had dinner yet?"

"No, I came straight here from the shoot with the dog."

"You have plans for dinner?" Colin asked.

"Chewing it," she responded. Heather giggled.

"How about if you do that chewing here?" Colin nodded at the puppy. "You might be in good company for that."

"Are you inviting me to dinner?" Ellie asked him.

His smile was slow and all the more sensual because it took its time. "Apparently."

"Then yes," she said as if she actually had a choice rather than finding herself held in place by that smile on his lips, "I'll stay."

The dog yipped even as Heather cried, "Yay!"

Colin nodded. "I guess it's unanimous, then," he told Ellie as he turned to walk into the kitchen. "Hope you're not starving," he added. "This might take a while."

Chapter Nine

"What are you making for dinner?" Ellie asked, following him into the kitchen. "Maybe I can help."

Colin removed a flyer he'd mounted on the refrigerator before turning round to face her.

"No, I've got it covered," he said, holding up the flyer. "Dialing the phone is pretty much a one-person activity."

"You're calling for takeout?" she asked him in surprise.

"Yes. Pizza," he specified. "Why? What'd you think?"

"Well, I thought you meant that you were going to cook it since you said it was going to take a while," Ellie answered.

"So does delivery after I make the call," he pointed out.

She debated just bowing out and letting him make his call. It was the simplest thing to do. But since he'd extended an invitation to her, she felt almost obligated to help out.

"Is your heart set on pizza?" she asked.

"Not particularly, but the wait time for pizza is the shortest and there's a Pizza King's less than a mile away," he pointed out, indicating the flyer in his hand.

Ellie moved past him and opened his refrigerator. She did a quick inventory of its contents—not exactly teeming, but not barren, either—then moved on to his rather limited pantry. That *was* relatively barren except for an unopened container of flavored bread crumbs and a few miscellaneous spices, origin unknown.

"Give me a few minutes," she told him. Then, looking up because she sensed he hadn't moved an inch, she said, "Go play with the puppy."

"What are you going to do?" he asked. The way he saw it, there wasn't very much to work with in either the refrigerator or the pantry. Just exactly what did she have in mind?

Ellie merely smiled and answered, "Make magic. Now go. Magic doesn't happen if you're watching for it."

Colin shook his head. The woman didn't look it at first, but she really was rather stubborn.

"Whatever you say. You change your mind and want to bail, here's the number of the pizza place," Colin told her, returning the flyer to the refrigerator and securing it with a magnet one of the real estate brokers had left on his doorstep.

"I won't be needing it," Ellie told him, pushing up her sleeves.

He had to admit he was enjoying this. "You sound very sure of yourself."

She spared him one last look before she shooed him out of the kitchen. "I am. Now go watch your niece play with the puppy."

He had no recourse but to do as she said.

"This was in my refrigerator?" Colin questioned less than half an hour later as he sat at the table with his niece and Ellie.

For the puppy's part, Pancakes had assumed an alert position between him and Heather, waiting for something to fall on the floor by either accident or design. Gifted with a strong sense of smell, as all dogs were, the puppy was already salivating.

"And your pantry," Ellie added. "In rough form," she allowed, "but it was definitely there."

"And what's this we're eating called again?" he asked.

"She said it was a frittata," Heather told him with the confidence of youth.

He got a kick out of the knowing way she'd answered him. "Oh, and you know what that is."

"Sure." She turned toward Ellie with a smile. "It's what we're eating, right, Ellie?"

"You're supposed to call her Ms. King," Colin corrected his niece.

Ellie had never been a stickler for formality and this whole evening was anything but formal. "I think we've come to the point where she can call me Ellie," the reporter told him. "And for the record, you can make a frittata as long as you have a few eggs and bread crumbs. The rest of the ingredients are really dealer's choice. You mix together a little meat, a few chopped-up vegetables, add in a little salt, a little cheese, maybe some mustard and you really *can't* mess things up. The ingredients kind of take care of each other."

"This is really good," Heather enthused. The girl looked hopefully at her new idol. "Can you teach me how to make it?"

"Anytime," Ellie told her.

Colin had eaten his first portion with gusto. A second helping gave him more time to actually examine what it was he was putting into his mouth.

"This is kind of like an omelet," Colin said after a moment.

"I'd prefer to think of it as an omelet's second cousin once removed," Ellie interjected. "It's in the family and related, but really not the same thing," she qualified.

"Where'd you learn how to make that?" Heather asked.

The answer came out before Ellie could stop the words or think to rechannel them into something less telling. Something that didn't open up a door that was supposed to remain shut.

"My husband taught me."

Colin and Heather both looked at her sharply, and Heather was the first to speak. "You're married?" she asked, appearing to soak up information about her role model like a sponge.

"I was," Ellie answered quietly, her trademark sunniness temporarily missing.

Colin continued staring at her, his attention caught by her subdued voice. Something distant stirred in his head and then the next moment, it faded into the background before he could snare it long enough to examine it.

"What happened?" Heather asked.

"Heather, that's not any of our business," Colin rebuked her.

But it was yours, Ellie thought, eyeing the detective.

Out loud she told Heather, "He died trying to defend some people."

There was an enormous amount of compassion and sympathy in the young face as Heather looked at her. "Was he a policeman like Uncle Colin?"

"No, he was a Marine," Ellie told her. "Anyone for seconds?" she asked, abruptly changing the subject and her tone of voice, going from somber to cheerful although she had to force the latter.

Heather pushed her plate forward. "Yes, please." And then she added in a lower voice, "I gave some of the frittata to Pancakes."

"I had a feeling," Ellie told her with a knowing nod. "You?" she asked, turning toward Colin.

"Sure, why not?" Colin responded gamely.

While she'd had to mix together a potpourri of ingredients for the main course, there was no lack for dessert. Olga had brought over a cherry pie last night and over half of it was still in the pie tin, waiting on their pleasure.

"Is Olga a relative?" Ellie asked, curious as to the dynamics that were involved since he'd already told her that the neighbor could be called upon to stay with Heather whenever he had to take off on a case. Apparently, the woman also seemed to be in the habit of dropping off baked goods and main courses, as well.

"No," Colin told her, getting three dessert plates.

Ellie took out three forks and one large knife. "Just a good neighbor."

"Uh-huh." She presented Colin with the knife, leaving the portion size up to him. "How old is this good neighbor?" Ellie asked.

"Why?" After cutting what was left in half, he divided that up into thirds.

Ellie shrugged. "Well, I wouldn't want the woman thinking that I'm trying to muscle in on her territory," she said.

"Oh no, Olga doesn't think like that," Heather assured her before her uncle could say anything. "Besides, Olga's really, really old."

Ellie laughed at the emphasis in Heather's voice. She could distinctly remember being that young only a little while ago. "What's old to you?" she asked, then took a guess. "Forty?"

Heather shook her head, sending the ends of her hair whipping about her face as if they'd been caught up in the wind. "No, even more than that."

"Olga's like the grandmother I never had," Colin clarified as the puppy all but ran up his side. "Although she does tend to move around rather quickly," he added. There was admiration in his voice. "I thought she was retired until she told me that she worked for a housecleaning service. She offered to clean my place for free."

"Why?" Ellie asked, gazing around. "Your place looks pretty clean to me."

"That's because Uncle Colin and I cleaned it up right after she said that," Heather volunteered.

Cherry-pie dessert consumed, the little girl was the first one down on the floor, lying flat on her back as her new pet walked along her stomach before losing her footing and falling off in a light tan heap.

Rather than remain seated at the table, Colin joined his niece. He grinned now, listening to Heather's delighted laugh as she played with Pancakes.

Picking up the conversation's thread, he said, "I figured if the woman was actually offering to clean my place for free, it had to be really bad. So Heather and I got busy and cleaned it up."

Not wanting to be left out, Ellie joined them on the floor. They looked like they were having a great deal of fun.

Colin's self-discipline in the face of his neighbor's offer impressed her. "Most men would have just taken her up on her offer instead of doing what you did," Ellie told him.

Reaching out, she scratched Pancakes behind her ears. The puppy whirled around to look at her and tripped over her own oversize paws. The next moment, she was picking herself up as if nothing had happened, her boundless energy still very much intact.

"Wouldn't seem right," Colin said truthfully, going on to say, "I don't know why I let it get out of hand like that." He shrugged. "Sometimes it just takes seeing a thing through someone else's eyes to make you realize what's wrong." As he said it, something seemed to click in his head again. And then, just like before, it was gone.

Ellie saw the pensive expression that momentarily came over his face. "You've got a strange look on your face," she observed.

"You ever have a thought that insists on playing

hide-and-seek with your brain, turning up and just as you try to catch it, it vanishes?"

"Sure. Some people claim that's evidence of a past life," she told him, wondering if something was causing him to make the connection between the past and now. Not a past life, but just the past, as in two years ago.

Not wanting to get into it tonight—they'd all had a very nice evening and she didn't want it to end on a bad note—she added flippantly, "Me, I just call it stress. There's only so much you can crowd into your brain and hope to retrieve it."

Colin wasn't up to any deep soul-searching tonight, so he shrugged. "You're probably right."

Ellie smiled, more to herself than at him. "I usually am," she replied. And then she glanced at her watch. It was late. Later than she'd anticipated.

She quickly got to her feet. "I'd better go—it's getting late."

Heather scrambled up with ease, all while clutching the puppy against her.

"Oh, do you have to?" she cried. "Can't you stay longer?" she begged.

"I stay any longer and I'll have to move in," Ellie quipped.

Heather took the remark and ran with it, turning to her uncle to ask, "Can she, Uncle Colin? Then she could be the one to bring me to school and—"

"No, honey, I was just kidding," Ellie hurried to say, setting the record straight.

The little girl sounded as if she could just keep extrapolating on the topic until she was adopting her by evening's end. Ellie wanted to save the detective from the awkward situation of explaining why he couldn't have an almost perfect stranger moving in. That "talk" was something she assumed the detective would save until such time as he had a girlfriend who wanted to move in with him.

Where the hell had that come from? Ellie silently demanded. And why in heaven's name was she even *thinking* of something like that? It wasn't any business of hers what the detective did—and with whom.

This was all just a short interlude in their lives, in *her* life, nothing more, Ellie insisted. There was no reason to make anything more of it than it already was—which was nothing. They were barely friends, much less anything more.

"Sorry," she said to Colin, apologizing that her thoughtless comment had caused what she assumed was a moment of discomfort on his part. "Now I'd *really* better be going."

Colin looked a little perplexed. "Nothing to be sorry about," he told the woman, puzzled as to why she would even say something like that. "I'm the one who probably should apologize. We've kept you much too long," he said.

Some of the tension drained from her. Ellie laughed, then held up her wrists.

"Yes, please remove the chains so that I can be on my way." The next moment she told him, "Let's just call it even. Nobody kept anybody and a very good time was had by all."

"Actually, you're right. Heather had a ball and I had a good time, too," he said, realizing that it was true. He looked down at the puppy, who looked like trouble that was about to happen. "Of course, if Pancakes winds up destroying anything really important, I'm sending you the bill."

Ellie nodded her head. "Fair enough."

They were at the door but something within Colin was reluctant to have it end just yet. He wanted a few more minutes with the woman.

He glanced over his shoulder toward his niece. Heather was back on the floor, bonding with the puppy, who was finally losing a tiny bit of her steam.

"I'm just going to walk Ellie to her car," he called out. "You two will be all right?"

"Sure," Heather piped up. "Pancakes'll take care of me."

"I'm not so sure about that," Colin confided to the woman next to him. "If anything it's the other way around."

"You're probably right," Ellie agreed. Then, because she didn't want to put him out, she said, "You don't have to walk me to my car. I'm parked just a few feet away."

"Then it'll be a short walk," he replied.

Ellie had always been one to choose her arguments. Arguing over something so minor seemed pointless, so she just went along with him.

Checking his pocket for his keys, Colin pulled the ground-floor-apartment door closed behind him. Looking around the immediate parking area, he asked, "Where's your car?"

She pointed to her light blue sedan. It was parked right in front of the rental office.

"It's not *that* close," he commented.

"But it's not in the next state, either," she countered.

"Humor me," he told her, shortening his gait until

it matched hers. "I'm a cop. Most cops are obsessed with safety."

"South Bedford doesn't strike me as being a very dangerous area."

As a local reporter, she would have heard something to the contrary if that was the case. As it was, the city was known as one of the very safest of its size in the country.

"It's not," he agreed. "But there's always a first time."

Ellie merely nodded as she said, "Uh-huh."

"Now you're humoring me."

"It's what you told me to do, remember?" she reminded him.

A minimum of steps, no matter how slowly taken, brought her to her sedan.

"Well, here we are," she announced, "at my car. Nice and safe," she added.

The rental office was closed for the night; all its lights but one were turned off. Night, with its autumn chill, had descended. She should have brought a sweater, Ellie thought. The temperature drop at night this time of year could be drastic.

"Cold?" he asked, noticing that she was trying unsuccessfully not to shiver.

"I'll be inside my car in a second," she told him.

He took that as a yes and was tempted to put his arm around her for momentary warmth.

Colin refrained and instead stepped back as she unlocked the driver-side door.

"You're still using a key," he observed.

She laughed at herself, admitting, "I'm old-fashioned. A key makes me feel like I'm in charge."

FREE Merchandise is 'in the Cards' for you!

Dear Reader,

We're giving away FREE MERCHANDISE!

Seriously, we'd like to reward you for reading this novel by giving you **FREE MERCHANDISE** worth over $20 retail. And no purchase is necessary!

You see the Jack of Hearts sticker above? Paste that sticker in the box on the Free Merchandise Voucher inside. Return the Voucher today… and we'll send you Free Merchandise!

Thanks again for reading one of our novels—and enjoy your Free Merchandise with our compliments!

Pam Powers

Pam Powers

P.S. Look inside to see what Free Merchandise is **"in the cards"** for you!

We'd like to send you two free books like the one you are enjoying now. Your two books have a combined price of over $10 retail, but they are yours to keep absolutely FREE! We'll even send you 2 wonderful surprise gifts. You can't lose!

REMEMBER: Your Free Merchandise, consisting of **2 Free Books** and **2 Free Gifts**, is worth over $20 retail! No purchase is necessary, so please send for your Free Merchandise today.

Get TWO FREE GIFTS!
We'll also send you 2 wonderful FREE GIFTS (worth about $10 retail), in addition to your 2 Free books!

Visit us at:
www.ReaderService.com

Books received may not be as shown.

"Is that important to you?" he asked. "Being in charge?"

"Sometimes," she acknowledged. "Other times," she allowed honestly, "not so much."

"I'm sorry if the conversation got a little too personal back there," Colin apologized, referring to the questions his niece had asked. "Heather tends to ask a lot of questions."

"Yes, I know, but that's all right," she said a little too quickly. "She has an inquisitive mind. Maybe she'll make a good reporter someday," Ellie speculated.

The conversation faded, its last strains drowned out by the sound of crickets making noise, each searching for a mate to spend the long night with.

There was a full moon out and as Colin looked on, it bathed Ellie in its light. As she turned to tell him good-night, Colin felt a very strong pull in the center of his gut.

At one point in his life, he would have just gone with it rather than trying to analyze it. But those times were behind him.

Or so he'd thought.

Despite Ellie's bravado, he couldn't shake the impression she gave him of a delicate, frightened doe that had to be approached with caution. Otherwise she'd take off.

The last thing he wanted to do was scare her off.

But the first thing he wanted to do, he realized with unmistakable clarity, was kiss her.

Chapter Ten

It was as if the world had suddenly, inexplicably slowed down to a crawl and everything from that point on was happening in slow motion.

There were only a couple of feet between Ellie and him, but they were eliminated not rapidly but almost a fraction of an inch at a time.

Colin drew closer; their faces drew nearer, ever nearer. Maybe he was imagining things, but he was almost certain that some of the distance between them, small as it was, was dispensed with by Ellie.

And then, at the final moment, just before his mouth came down on hers, Colin gave up thinking altogether. He just surrendered to the ever-growing attraction that had been between them all along.

He gave her ample time to stop him or turn away if she wanted to.

She didn't.

When Ellie didn't pull away or protest, he deepened the kiss and then put his arms around her to draw her even closer to him.

Colin hadn't fully realized how much he'd wanted this until just now, until it was actually happening. And it wasn't that he missed the experience and just wanted to kiss an attractive woman. He really wanted to kiss *her*, Elliana King.

When he felt Ellie threading her arms around his neck while they were still kissing, something within him cheered and he could have sworn he saw fireworks going off in his head.

At least it seemed that way.

It had been so long, so very long, since she'd let herself feel like a woman. She'd forgotten how really wondrous it could feel. Adrenaline raced through her, heightening her reaction. Everything within her pleaded "More" as she felt Colin deepen the kiss, making her literally ache.

Making her remember.

Everything inside Ellie sped up. Her breathing, her pulse, her reaction. Colin's arms enfolded her, pulling her closer, all but making her a part of him.

Colin's arms felt strong.

He made her feel safe.

Her defenses melted away.

And then the alarms in her head went off.

She was wrong.

She wasn't safe. She'd *never* be safe—she knew that. Pain was always just a heartbeat away, waiting to dismantle her, to consume her. Her only defense was not to allow herself to feel anything, not ever again. She couldn't set herself up for another fall, another heartache. This time, when, not *if*, it happened, it would completely destroy her.

At the same time guilt flooded through her, guilt over betraying Brett's memory. Brett was gone and she was alive. After two years it still made no sense to her. She didn't understand how she could keep on drawing breath in a world where he no longer was.

Appalled at what she'd just allowed to happen, what she was *guilty* of doing, Ellie suddenly braced her hands against the muscular chest that had been only a moment ago pressed against hers and she pushed Colin away with all her might.

"No," she cried, pulling her head back. "I can't. I'm sorry. I can't."

The words tumbled out over each other. She struggled not to break down in sobs as she quickly got into her vehicle.

In her hurry to escape, Ellie didn't even buckle her seat belt when she drove away. She left a stunned Colin in her wake.

"What the hell just happened here?" Colin murmured to himself, completely confused.

He hadn't a clue.

But he damn well intended to find out. He stood there for a moment, trying to figure out what had just transpired. Trying to understand why she'd been so warm and pliable in his arms one moment and then bolting like a bat out of hell that had been set on fire the next.

Turning around, he headed back to his apartment. Someone else would have just chalked up what had occurred to flaky behavior, but Colin wasn't the type who put much stock in those kinds of one-size-fits-all labels.

And even if he were, Ellie King just wasn't that kind of person. By no stretch of the imagination could she be regarded as "flaky."

Something else was at the bottom of this.

The whole incident was still very much on his mind the next morning.

Could he have misread the signals she'd been giving off, he asked himself. He wasn't usually wrong when it came to making judgment calls about people, either on the job or off.

No, something else was going on and he needed to find out what if he was to ever have any peace of mind about this.

He needed to get to the station to do some research.

To that end, he wanted to leave early. As with everything else in his life since he'd become a guardian, it required multiple steps.

He convinced Heather to hustle, not an easy accomplishment when all his niece really wanted to do was stay home and play with her new pet, all the while talking about what a great person Elliana King was.

Even as he got his niece out the door early, it didn't end there. He had the puppy to consider. For the sake of the rest of his furniture, he put a bowl of the dog food that Ellie had brought plus a bowl of water into the bathroom and closed the door.

Pitiful whining began almost instantly.

"Pancakes is going to think we're punishing her,"

Heather lamented even as he steered his niece through the doorway and out of the apartment.

He'd already noticed teeth marks on the corner molding by the kitchen.

"No, I did that so we don't *have* to punish her when we get home tonight." He opened the car's doors. "I'll pick up a puppy crate today," he promised. "Problem solved."

Heather climbed into the car, automatically reaching for her seat belt and buckling up.

"A crate?" she cried in dismay. "You're going to lock Pancakes up in a box?" she wailed indignantly.

"Actually, I heard somewhere that dogs like being in a crate—it's like their own little cave, their own space to defend." Backing out of his parking space, Colin saw the dubious way his niece looked at him. "I'm not making this up, Heather. It's on the internet," he told her. "Look it up."

Since they both knew that she was far more proficient on the computer than he was and could easily check out what he was telling her, that seemed to placate her, at least for now.

He only wished that the problem with Ellie could be so easily resolved, Colin thought ruefully.

The root of the problem, he decided after he'd dropped Heather off at school, had to be with Ellie's husband. She'd told Heather that he'd died. Maybe the woman had unresolved feelings about his death, or even more likely, she felt disloyal being attracted to another man.

No ego failing to thrive here, Colin thought, mocking himself.

In order to begin to understand why things had suddenly gone south last night, he would have to educate himself about the woman he found himself so attracted to.

The good news, he thought as he walked into the squad room, was that everyone's life was an open book to some extent these days. While he himself had little time for that—the tools of social media just did *not* interest him—he knew that others did.

Nowadays everyone in the public eye, celebrities, politicians, actors, newscasters, all of those people, depended on having a following—obviously the more the better for the purposes of their careers. Which in turn meant that Elliana King's life had to be accessible to him.

Colin decided, at least to start with, to go the easy route, so he just did a search on her name.

There was no shortage of sources.

He highlighted the first websites in the list, forgoing various videos, reviews and the comments written in by others. He wasn't interested in what anyone else thought of her. What he wanted to find out about was Ellie's background. Not the name of the station where she got her start, or what schools she graduated from—that was information to look into on possibly another day. He was specifically interested in the fleeting comment Ellie had made to his niece when Heather had asked her if she was married.

He had a feeling that the answers he was seeking and her abrupt about-face last night could be found there. Unearthing her bio didn't take him long. He waded through paragraphs of information until he got to the crucial part.

As he was reading, the muscles in his jaw slack-ened. He read the pertinent paragraphs he'd found several times to make sure he hadn't misread them.

And then he went into his own back files. Specifi-cally, the last case he'd had as a uniformed officer.

It all came back to him.

"Damn it, that's why," he muttered.

"Why what?" Sanchez asked, looking up. Coming in late, Al Sanchez had just put down his coffee con-tainer and pulled up his chair.

Their desks butted up against one another and Colin now looked across that expanse. He hadn't realized he'd said anything out loud. Glancing up, he locked eyes with the man he'd only recently been partnered with. His old partner had switched departments at the same time that Sanchez's partner had retired. Theirs was not a marriage made in heaven, but it was com-fortable enough and growing more so.

"Nothing," Colin murmured.

"Sounded like a pretty loud 'nothing' to me," San-chez contradicted. "Give." When Colin made no re-sponse, Sanchez got up from his desk and circled around behind his new partner. "We catch a cold case?" he asked, reading the information on the screen.

Rather than close the window, Colin decided to leave it open. Sanchez was the type to keep digging once his interest was aroused.

"No, it's a closed case," Colin said. "My last case as a uniformed officer. A convenience-store robbery that went wrong." He recalled it now as vividly as if it had happened yesterday.

Sanchez read a few lines and began to nod. "Yeah, I remember that one. That's the one with the Marine who'd just come home after a couple of tours of duty. He tried to stop this guy from robbing a young couple and caught a bullet for his trouble."

Colin turned his seat to look at his partner, curious. "Why would you remember this case?"

"Because of that reporter on the local news station, the woman who was covering it. She fainted on the air and that created a hell of a stir. Didn't you see it?" Sanchez asked, surprised.

Colin shook his head. "No."

Back in those days, he never even turned on the TV monitor in his apartment. He'd been too busy enjoying the company of the fairer sex to spend his time watching images on the screen.

"Why'd did she faint?" Colin asked. The tingling feeling he was experiencing told him that he might just be onto why Ellie had reacted the way she had last night.

Sanchez blew out a breath. "Well, it seems that no one told her that the guy who saved that couple at the convenience store from being shot—and got killed for his trouble—was her husband," he recalled.

Colin could only stare at his partner. "What?"

Sanchez nodded. "Yeah. He'd only been home a couple of days and was just picking up a carton of milk on his way home when he saw what was going down and put himself in harm's way to keep that young couple from getting hurt. The robber panicked and started shooting. That was *your* case?" Sanchez asked in disbelief. He shook his head in amazement. "Small world, I guess."

"Too small," was all that Colin would say.

It explained a lot.

What it didn't explain was why Ellie hadn't said anything to him. She had to have known of his involvement in the case. He was the officer on record and if she'd covered the story, she had to know that he was the policeman who'd taken down the killer—and the one who'd tried to save her husband.

Tried and failed, Colin reminded himself grimly. He could still see the Marine's blood oozing through his fingers as he vainly applied pressure to the wound to try to stop the bleeding.

Damn it, Colin thought in frustration, that was what had been nagging at him all this time, what kept trying to surface only to fade away again. This was that elusive memory that refused to take shape, the one he kept trying to catch hold of but just couldn't.

Why hadn't Ellie said anything to him? he asked himself again in exasperation. When she'd first shown up at the station to do that interview with him, she must have known then who he was. She'd said that she'd done her homework—that meant getting his background. She was far too much of a professional not to have known the connection between them.

And yet she hadn't said anything.

Why?

Colin felt confused, conflicted.

His mind peeled apart the situation in a dozen different ways with none of them yielding a satisfactory conclusion. About the only thing he knew at this point was that he needed to collect himself before he talked to Ellie about it.

Right now he felt like someone who had just walked over a land mine. He was still intact, but just barely—and very likely to say the wrong thing.

Wanting to distract himself—and calm down—Colin used his lunch hour to go to the pet store to purchase the puppy crate he'd told his niece about. While he was at it, he stocked up on several different kinds of dog treats and another bag of dry dog food, this one manufactured by a chef who prided herself on being able to prepare food equally appetizing for man and beast.

He dropped all that off, along with a couple of chew toys that he thought might come in handy, in his apartment.

Colin remained there only long enough to release Pancakes from the bathroom and place the puppy into her new home away from home, the puppy crate. He felt that the puppy needed to get accustomed to it before Heather came home.

Once he finally got back to the station, Colin called Olga, leaving a detailed message on her answering machine about both the puppy and the new crate, explaining everything.

He fervently hoped the woman liked dogs.

The remainder of the time that he spent at the station, Colin focused on work, giving it his undivided attention. Apparently, the witless art thief he'd caught the other day—the one that had brought Ellie into his life—wanted to make a deal with the assistant DA. The latter had said that his presence was needed to verify and back up several facts of the case.

While Colin always invested himself in his job 100 percent, he couldn't block out the thoughts about Ellie that were at the back of his mind, slowly eating away at him.

For that reason, Colin couldn't wait for his day to

finally be over. He just prayed that nothing would come up at the last minute, the way it was wont to do at times, necessitating his presence beyond the end of his shift.

The second his shift was officially over, Colin cleared out, his hasty exodus causing his partner to comment rather wistfully, "Hot date tonight?"

"I wouldn't describe it as that," Colin answered, not wanting to go into specifics.

Sanchez locked his drawer and shrugged into his plaid jacket.

"Hell, I'd settle for a lukewarm date at this point. All the wife and I do is stare at the TV—separately," he emphasized. "She's got hers on in the living room, I watch my shows in the family room."

He and Sanchez walked out of the squad room together. "Maybe you should give watching together a try," Colin suggested.

Sanchez merely shook his head at the idea. He pressed for the elevator. "She doesn't like any of the programs I watch."

"Try watching the ones she likes," Colin told the older man.

Sanchez made a face as they got on the elevator car. "I'm not that desperate," he told his partner as the doors closed.

Some horses just couldn't be led to water. "Think about why you proposed to her in the first place."

In response, Sanchez rolled his eyes dramatically. "*That* hasn't happened in a long time."

He was definitely getting too much information

here, Colin thought. He had only one last suggestion for his romance-challenged partner.

"Maybe if you watch TV with her, it might. You'll never know until you try," he told the man.

Reaching the ground floor, the elevator opened and they both got off.

"Yeah, well, maybe. We'll see," Sanchez muttered. "See you in the morning."

"Right, see you."

They parted company at the front door.

Colin hurried over to his sedan.

He had suppressed the urge to call Ellie more than a dozen times today, feeling that a face-to-face meeting with her would be far more effective than just talking to her on the phone.

He considered his options. He did *not* want to confront her at work and turning up at her home might make the woman feel he was stalking her. So the only thing left for him to do was sit in his car in the studio's parking lot and wait for her to leave the building where she worked. She had to come out sometime.

As it turned out, he didn't have long to wait.

Chapter Eleven

Ellie's heart almost stopped when she spotted Colin walking toward her. Acutely aware of the way they had parted last night, she would have preferred pretending that she didn't see him, but he had seen her looking right at him, so there was no way she could avoid saying something to him.

However, she didn't want to get into any sort of a serious discussion, either. Doing so would just bring up memories that hurt far too much.

Momentarily at a loss as to how to handle the situation, Ellie said the first thing that came to her mind.

"Something wrong with the puppy?"

"The puppy's fine. My apartment's a little worse for the wear, but I picked up a puppy crate at a pet store, so that should keep her from chewing up everything in sight while I'm not home."

"Good," Ellie said, not really listening. All she wanted to do was get away. Reaching her car, she began to open the driver-side door. "If there's nothing else, I've got to be—"

Colin didn't put his hand up to keep the door from closing, didn't block her access to it with his body. It was what he said that caused her to freeze in place. "Why didn't you tell me?"

The same heart that had felt as if it stopped beating at the sight of him now seemed to sink all the way down into her stomach. Obviously, she wasn't going to be able to make that quick getaway.

"You didn't come to see me about the puppy, did you?" she asked quietly.

She couldn't read his expression. "No, I didn't." His eyes pinned her in place as surely as if someone had nailed her shoes to the ground. And then the detective surprised her with a question. "We've interacted how many times?"

She braced herself for a confrontation. Jerry had warned her about this and he was right, she couldn't help thinking. She should have told Colin about the way they were connected before this.

Ellie shrugged. She wanted to look away, but she didn't and wanted to defend her position if she could.

"I don't know," she told him. "Honestly, I wasn't counting."

"Five," he answered in the same emotionless voice he'd just used. "Five times if you count when you interviewed me on camera and my phone call after that piece aired. We interacted *five* times and not once could you tell me that you knew that I was the one who found your husband at the convenience store that night. Why?" Colin demanded.

Ellie shrugged again, feeling helpless. Feeling cornered. She hated it, even if ultimately Benteen had a point. She *should* have told him. She hadn't. End of story.

"There was no right way to work it into the conversation."

"The hell with the 'right way,'" he told her, raising his voice as he dismissed what he viewed as flawed reasoning. "How about the right thing?" he asked. "As in telling me you knew I was the cop on record that night. How could you keep something like that from me?" he demanded, struggling to control his temper. "Were you planning on springing it on me after you were convinced that I was hooked on you? Did you want to make me somehow pay for not being able to save him?" Colin asked. "Because I tried, Ellie. I tried my damnedest to save him and it haunted me for a long time that I couldn't."

She stared at him, speechless.

"I rode all the way to the hospital in the ambulance with him, trying to bully him into hanging on even when I knew there was no hope," he told her.

Colin blew out a breath, his impotent anger beginning to subside. "I didn't know you found out about his death while you were on the air, doing the story about the foiled robbery. I had no idea until Sanchez informed me today," he said. "Maybe I should have been the one to notify you about his death, but my sergeant told me someone was sent to talk to the Marine's family, and frankly, I was glad because I didn't want to have to face them. I didn't want to tell them that I couldn't save him."

"There was no 'family,'" Ellie informed him in a still, subdued voice. "There was only me."

His eyes continued to hold hers. "And you knew I was the patrolman?" he asked her.

Ellie nodded her head slowly. "Yes, I knew," she admitted.

"Then why didn't you say something?" he asked. "I don't mean when you had that microphone shoved in my face, but afterward, why didn't you tell me you knew who I was?"

He wanted to know, okay, she'd tell him, Ellie decided—and hoped that she wouldn't wind up breaking down while she did it. "Because I didn't want to bring it up. Because I'm still trying to put it behind me." There were tears in her eyes as she looked at him. Tears she was desperately struggling to hold back. "Because it was all my fault."

That was a curveball he hadn't expected. For a second, she'd knocked the air out of him. And then he found his tongue.

"How was it your fault?"

She gave up trying not to cry. The tears slid down her cheeks. "If I hadn't told him to pick up that damn quart of milk on his way home, he wouldn't have stopped at the convenience store. And if he hadn't stopped, he'd still be alive."

"Was he passing the convenience store on his way home?"

"Yes," she answered, averting her face so he couldn't watch her crying.

Colin took her face in his hands and deliberately

but gently turned it toward him. "Then he would have seen the robbery taking place and, being the kind of man he was, he would have tried to stop it anyway."

Seeing Ellie crying this way undid him completely. Colin took her into his arms and held her. "It wasn't the milk, it was the man, and ultimately you had nothing to do with that."

Ellie resisted his offer of comfort for all of thirty seconds. And then she just broke down and really cried. Cried the way she hadn't allowed herself to cry in two years.

She cried for a long time.

Colin said nothing. Instead, he held her, letting her cry it out, his silence telling her that he was there for her if she needed him. That all he wanted her to do was feel better.

Finally, spent, Ellie drew her head back. "Oh God," she said, trying to wipe away the tears from her cheeks with her hands. "I must look like such a mess."

Colin smiled as he offered her his handkerchief. "A beautiful mess," he amended.

She took his handkerchief. "Right. You must have a very low threshold of *beautiful*," Ellie told him as she passed his handkerchief along first one cheek, then the other, drying them in earnest before she handed the handkerchief back to him.

"Actually, I don't." Colin absently tucked the cloth into his pocket. His attention was completely focused on her. "Do you feel like going somewhere for a drink?" he asked.

"A cop encouraging drinking and driving?" she asked wryly, doing her best to smile. It was a half-hearted effort at best.

"Doesn't have to be alcohol," he pointed out, then offered her some choices. "Coffee? Tea? Maybe a smoothie?"

Ellie eyed him rather skeptically and asked in disbelief, "You drink smoothies?"

He laughed softly, understanding her surprise. He wouldn't have touched a smoothie six months ago, but things had changed since then.

"Actually, I've tried a lot of things since I became Heather's guardian," he told her. "She loves them and I have to admit, some of them aren't half bad. How about it?"

She took another deep breath, trying to steady herself. "Speaking of Heather, shouldn't you be getting home to her?"

"It's okay," he assured her. "Olga's watching her. And now that she's got Pancakes, I don't think Heather even notices I'm not there."

"Oh, she notices," Ellie assured him, more attuned to his niece than he thought. "Trust me, with her parents gone, you're the center of her universe."

This time as she opened her car door in order to slide in behind the steering wheel, Colin did hold the door in place. She looked up at him, waiting for an explanation. She'd assumed that they were done; obviously not.

"You shouldn't be alone right now," he told her seriously. "Tell you what—why don't you follow me home?"

A refusal was on the tip of her tongue, but she knew he was right. She really didn't want to be alone tonight. After what had just happened here, if she was alone, it would give her time to think and magnify everything.

She supposed she could always call her mother. Her mother would be over before she had time to terminate her call. She knew that her mother worried about her. Her mother especially worried about her not getting on with her life and she didn't want to have that conversation tonight.

Colin was still watching her, waiting for an answer to his suggestion that she follow him home. Waiting for her to agree.

"I bet you say that to all the women," she said flippantly.

"Actually," he told her, his eyes still on hers, "I don't." The next moment, he deliberately lightened the mood by asking her another question. "Don't you want to see what that energized ball of fur is doing to my floorboards?" When she seemed confused, he elaborated on the situation. "I didn't know that dogs teethed."

"Well, she's a puppy, which means she's a baby dog, and all babies teethe, so I guess it's to be expected."

He supposed she was right. But just like he'd never been a guardian before, he'd also never had a pet before. This was all just one giant learning process for him.

"A little warning might have been nice," Colin told her.

"Think of it as a learn-as-you-go kind of situation," she suggested.

"Do I have a choice?" he asked, knowing that he didn't. Heather was so crazy about the dog there was no way the animal could be given its walking papers. Pancakes was there to stay.

Ellie laughed then. It was a small laugh, but in his estimation, it was gratifying to hear.

"No."

"Then I'll learn as I go," he said thoughtfully. "So, are we all set? You're following me home?" he asked, just to be clear that she hadn't changed her mind. "I know that Heather'll be thrilled."

Ellie nodded, relieved that she had an excuse. She wondered if Colin knew that.

"I can't disappoint my fan base, I guess," she agreed.

"Good," he pronounced, glad that *that* was settled. "Then I'll see you at the apartment."

As he turned to go, Ellie caught her lower lip between her teeth, debating. And then called after him just before he was out of earshot.

"Colin?"

He turned around thinking she was going to beg off after all, so he braced himself. In the end, the decision was up to her. He knew he couldn't very well drag her off by her hair. There was only so much persuading he could do.

"Yes?" Colin stood there, waiting.

She'd never had a problem with apologies. If she was wrong, she always willingly owned up to it. But this time around, it was hard. Hard for so many reasons. Now that it was out in the open, there was no turning back. It had to be done.

"I'm sorry I didn't tell you that I knew who you were right after the interview. Actually, after it happened— after Brett was killed—I did have every intention of finding you. I wanted to talk to you, to ask you questions. I wanted you to fill me in on Brett's last moments."

Since she hadn't tried to get in contact with him, he asked, "What happened?"

Ellie pressed her lips together. "I just couldn't make myself do it," she said honestly. "So I kept finding excuses and before I knew it, too much time had gone by and I felt awkward about opening up what had to be an old case for you."

That wasn't the whole truth and she knew it. Taking another breath, she told him, "I guess I felt that until I actually talked to you about Brett's last moments, I didn't have to deal with them myself. That way, the whole thing wasn't quite real to me." She flushed ruefully. "I guess you probably think that's stupid, don't you?"

Colin offered an understanding smile. "Actually, it happens more than you think."

She waved her hand at him, dismissing his words. "You're just saying that to make me feel better."

His face gave nothing away as he asked, "Is it working?"

It coaxed another smile from her. "I'll see you at your apartment," she told him.

"Okay," he agreed. "And if you're not there within ten minutes of my arriving home, I'm going to come looking for you."

"Duly warned," she responded, grateful that he had made this easy for her. Grateful that he hadn't just written her off as being a crazy woman with too much baggage for him to bother with.

The best way to handle this was not to think, Ellie told herself as she drove behind Colin's sedan. And she wasn't going to make too much of this. Benteen was just being a friend. She didn't want anything more than that.

Because if she *did* make it anything more than that, she would be setting herself up for another grievous fall fraught with pain. The man was a police detective, for heaven's sakes. Police detectives risked getting shot in the line of duty on a daily basis. She couldn't even allow herself to fall in love with a dentist and the only risk a dentist ran was possibly accidentally drilling his own fingers. The point was that most professions weren't being paid to face death on a regular basis.

A police detective was, so there couldn't be anything more between them than there was right at this moment.

That meant that she was just going over to spend some time with a friend, his niece and the overly energetic puppy she had gifted him with. Nothing else would happen.

Ever.

Granted, she had kissed him, but, she silently insisted, it was only to get that out of the way. Now that it was, she could go on without having to worry. Like Peter Pan, whose mantra was "I won't grow up," she lived by the mantra "I won't fall in love." And nothing would make her fall again.

Nothing.

When she arrived at the door to Colin's apartment some fifteen minutes later, she knocked once, mentally giving him to the count of ten before turning around to go back to her car. The drive over had waned her initial resolution to view this whole interaction between the sexy police detective and herself as something residing in the realm of playfully platonic. She was better off keeping her "interactions" to a minimum. "Minimum" did *not* include spending the evening with him, even with a dog and a niece between them as buffers.

Despite the pep talk to the contrary, she knew she was playing with fire.

Ellie was up to nine and ready to turn on her heel to leave when the door opened. She didn't know whether to cry or cheer.

But instead of Colin or his precocious, animated niece, Ellie found herself looking up at a rather tall, somewhat austere-looking older woman who wore her fading blond hair in what looked to be a braided crown woven about her head.

The next moment, she realized that this had to be Colin's next-door neighbor, Olga, the woman who offered to clean his house for free and who baked cherry pies to die for.

About to introduce herself—and possibly beg off—Ellie never got the chance to do either. The second the woman saw her, she caught her by the hand and enthusiastically pulled her into the apartment, declaring, "You must be the reporter lady," in an accent that was veritably thick enough to cut with a knife, preferably one that butchers used.

"I must be," Ellie heard herself replying as she all but flew over the threshold, not of her own accord. At the last moment, she steadied herself to keep from falling over.

Olga gave her a quick appraising look, apparently pleased with what she saw.

Olga smiled to herself.

"Your reporter lady is here," Olga announced, tossing the words over her shoulder and then adding, "And now I am not."

And just like that, the woman was gone.

Chapter Twelve

"I guess Olga approves of you," Colin told her.

Ellie turned around to find both the detective and his niece standing behind her. Heather was holding the puppy—or trying to. Pancakes seemed to have her own ideas about the situation and tried to use her hind legs to climb down the girl's body.

The older woman hadn't given her any indication that she liked her, Ellie thought. Had she missed something? "How do you know that?"

"Simple," Colin answered. "Because she let you in."

Ellie nodded, following Colin, Heather and their furry friend into the living room. "I guess she did look like she could physically block the doorway to keep me out if she wanted to."

Forgetting about Olga, Ellie turned toward Pancakes. The puppy was practically vibrating in her efforts to get free. Heather, however, had a tight grip on the dog, determined not to let her escape just yet.

"So, how's everything going with Pancakes?" Ellie asked. The words were no sooner out of her mouth than she noticed the chew marks along the floorboard where the two sides came together at the corner. "Wow, you weren't kidding about her teething, were you?"

Ellie bent down to get a better look at the damage. Apparently, Pancakes had gnawed away at the paint clear down to the drywall. "Some paint should take care of that," she told Colin, rising. "And then, after it dries, spray everything shin level and lower with bitter apple."

Colin would have been the first to admit that he didn't know all that much about painting walls, but he was fairly certain that bitter apples had nothing to do with it.

"Come again?"

"Pet stores carry it," Ellie told him, stroking the culprit as she continued to try to wiggle out of Heather's arms. "It's used mostly to keep dogs from chewing on themselves, but it'll probably do the same thing for the walls and your furniture if you spray them." She shrugged as she turned to look at him. "At least it won't hurt anything."

"Worth a shot," Colin agreed.

"Olga brought another one of her casseroles over, so you don't have to cook tonight," Heather announced with a grin, making it sound as if having Ellie prepare dinner was a regular occurrence rather than something that had happened just twice.

Ellie supposed that in the world of a ten-year-old, anything that had been done more than once fell under the heading of Routine.

Exchanging looks with Colin to make sure that his invitation to her was meant to include dinner—he nodded, so she assumed it did—Ellie answered, "Sounds good."

Heather planted herself directly in front of her. "I have to take Pancakes out for a walk so she can go to the bathroom. Wanna come?" she asked.

"Sounds even better," Ellie told her before Colin had the chance to tell his niece not to pester her. She could see the reprimand coming. "Really," she emphasized, looking at the detective.

Colin held his peace.

Serpentine patches of grass were woven all through the apartment-complex grounds, going around the various apartments and giving the development a rather rustic look reminiscent of the city's earlier days, before it was incorporated. Because of that, there was no shortage of places that Pancakes could stop and investigate. Investigation in this case consisted mainly of sniffing, sometimes so deeply that the dog wound up sneezing, something that in turn entertained Heather.

"I didn't know dogs could sneeze," she said.

"Pets are a constant source of education," Ellie told her.

"Did you have pets when you were my age?" Heather asked.

"My dad was allergic to anything with fur, so we couldn't have any pets in the house," she told the girl. "Other than a goldfish, of course, and that doesn't really count. You can't play with a goldfish," she added with a wink.

Heather giggled, then fell into silence for a moment before saying, "You can think of Pancakes as your dog, too, if you want."

Ellie slipped an arm around the little girl's shoulders and hugged Heather to her. "That's very generous of you." Heather beamed at her in response.

By the time she, Heather and the puppy returned to their starting point, Ellie felt a great deal more relaxed.

"I asked Ellie to come to my school for career day," Heather announced the moment they walked into the apartment.

In the kitchen warming up Olga's casserole, Colin stuck his head out and gave his niece a reproving look. "Heather, what did I tell you about that?"

Heather looked up at him innocently. "You said that Ellie was too busy to come to my classroom, but when I asked her, she said she wasn't."

Colin suppressed a frustrated sigh. It was a losing battle with Heather, so he turned to her target instead. "You don't have to do this, you know."

"I know. I already said yes," Ellie told him, taking the leash off Pancakes.

He knew how easily his niece could wrap him around her finger, but he couldn't allow her to do that to Ellie. "Heather's a hard person to say no to," he acknowledged, "but she can't expect you to just drop everything and talk to a class of ten-year-olds," he said, looking at Heather even though his words were directed at Ellie.

The crestfallen expression on Heather's face was enough to seal the fate of this dispute.

"That's okay," Ellie assured him. "They like this kind of thing at the station. They'll probably send Jerry to film it."

"Jerry?" Colin asked.

"My cameraman. You remember, big guy—" she held her hand up high "—curly hair."

Now he remembered. "Oh, right."

"I'm gonna be on TV?" Heather cried. She was already excited by the prospect of having Ellie come to speak to her class; having it all immortalized on film would send her over the top.

"We'll see how this goes," Ellie cautioned, not wanting Heather to get overly excited until the segment was approved. Turning to Colin, she told him, "She's got a lot in common with the puppy."

Colin merely sighed. "Tell me about it." And then he remembered the casserole he'd left on top of the stove. "Okay, let's eat before it all gets cold," he urged, ushering Ellie and his niece into the kitchen.

As she allowed herself to be brought into the kitchen, Ellie couldn't help thinking that it felt really nice being part of a family unit. She knew that it was just an illusion and only temporary, but she could still enjoy the moment and pretend that this was real.

Ellie wasn't exactly sure how it started, but a pattern seemed to begin forming, pulling her in almost without her being conscious of it.

Before she knew it, at least four, sometimes five, evenings a week would find her having dinner with Colin and his niece. Oh, there were various pretexts involved in this unfolding pattern—the first and foremost was that she had somehow gotten herself roped into helping Heather train the lively Pancakes. The goal, for everyone's sake, was to turn the ever-livelier puppy into if not an obedient pet, one who at least waited for her walk to relieve herself and who understood what the commands *sit* and *come* meant.

Ellie promised the little girl—and Colin—that more commands would come once Pancakes got those two down pat.

Training the dog took patience and perseverance and, most of all, a lot of man-hours, or in this case, woman-hours. Colin himself couldn't always be there, because the dictates of his job would call him away. Thieves, as he'd explained once to Heather, did not keep regular nine-to-five hours.

And there were times when Ellie was sent out to cover a late-breaking story. Calling Colin to make her apologies was particularly difficult whenever Heather answered the phone.

The preteen always sounded severely disappointed if she couldn't see her that evening. So much so that sometimes Ellie wondered if her absence even registered with Heather's uncle. That was when she reminded herself that they were just friends, nothing more, and there was no reason for him to be anywhere nearly as disappointed as Heather was.

After all, except for that one time, Colin hadn't even tried to kiss her again, so the parameters defining their relationship were clearly etched. They were friends, growing to be very good friends, but definitely nothing more than that.

She clung to the label for her own protection— even though at times it actually did really bother her.

"Tell me one thing," she said to Heather the morning before she addressed the girl's fourth-grade class on career day several weeks later. "Why am I here instead of your uncle? Aren't students supposed to bring a family member to these things?"

"Well, you're like family," Heather answered, saying it as if she believed that with every fiber of her being. "And anyway, you're a lot more famous than Uncle Colin is."

She didn't want the girl to get her priorities mixed up. Being famous wasn't everything. It should score very low on her list of aspirations.

"But your uncle's a police detective and that's very important, honey. The police keep our community safe."

"I know that," Heather said, dismissing the point the next moment. "But people see you on TV," she stressed. "Everybody in my class knows who you are. They all watch you," she said proudly.

Ellie gave it one more try. "Just remember, if you're ever in trouble, you call a policeman," she emphasized, "not a reporter."

Which was what she wound up telling her audience at the end of her presentation, hoping that the message registered with the class, although truthfully, she had her doubts. They all seemed far too interested in being on camera themselves.

She'd been right about her news station viewing this as a good opportunity to both promote some good publicity and get a feel-good human-interest story. Everyone wanted to know when the segment would air so they could tell their family and friends.

"So how did it go?" Colin asked that evening when he finally came home. His shift had run over. Consequently, he came home several hours after Ellie had arrived, relieving Olga.

"Your niece is a hit," Ellie told him.

"Everyone wants to be my friend now that I brought Ellie to school," she announced.

He looked at Heather, concerned about her feelings. "You know that's not going to last, right? They should want to be your friend because they like you, not because you know someone they see on TV."

"I know that. Ellie already explained that to me. But how are they going to know if they like me if they don't talk to me? Now they talk to me because I brought in Ellie."

"Hard to argue with logic like that," Ellie quipped. "If I were you, I'd start putting money aside for her college fund. This one's got the makings of a really good lawyer."

Colin laughed and shook his head. "Let's eat— I'm starved."

"Tonight's dinner is Hungarian goulash. Olga brought it over," Ellie told him. "She actually smiled at me today."

"Told you she liked you," Colin said, helping her set the table.

"Well, I wouldn't exactly go that far," Ellie countered. "But I think that Olga might be coming around since Heather told her that I went to her class for career day."

"See that?" Colin said. "A classroom of kids bests a dour Russian lady and you've got a classroom full of ten-year-olds idolizing you."

Ellie distributed the napkins at the three place settings. "That's just because they think being on camera is glamorous. They haven't seen the segments where I've had to stand out in the pouring rain, reporting on 'the storm of the century,' which turns out to be just three days of bad weather. Or the time the station had me reporting on the hurricane that was just off the coast," she recalled. "I looked like a wet rat."

He grinned, envisioning the scene. "A photogenic wet rat," Colin corrected.

That caught her off guard. Colin didn't usually compliment her. "You think I'm photogenic?"

He looked at her, amused. "You think you're not?" he countered.

"Actually," she confessed, "I haven't thought about it at all." She had to submit herself to the makeup woman daily, but she didn't bother looking to see what the final result was when the woman finished.

"Don't you look at yourself on TV?" Colin asked, surprised. Everyone he knew was keenly aware of how they looked. He'd always thought it was part of the human condition.

"No," Ellie answered with a dismissive shrug.

Heather was carefully putting glasses next to the place settings. She looked up at her idol in total surprise.

"Why not?" she asked. "If I was on TV, I'd watch me all the time."

"That's because you're adorable," Ellie told the preteen. "I feel too self-conscious. If I looked, I'd see all my flaws and all my mistakes."

"What if there aren't any?" Colin challenged.

"There are *always* mistakes," Ellie assured him, then deftly changed the subject. She was never comfortable talking about herself. "So, how was your day?"

"Frustrating," Colin said honestly. "There's been a rash of home invasions. So far, we haven't been able to catch who's behind them."

"What about descriptions?" she asked. Using a deep serving spoon, she doled out helpings on all three plates. "Home invasions mean that the people were at home at the time, right? Can't any of the people who were robbed give you an accurate description of the thieves?" Finished serving, she sat down and began to eat.

"They come in wearing masks and tie the people up, blindfolding them. We're not even getting an accurate count of how many home invaders there are. One couple said two—another said four. Nobody's agreeing with each other."

"Could be that there are several teams," Ellie suggested. "All working for one head guy—or woman," she amended. "What about surveillance tapes? Almost everyone has home security systems these days, or at least cameras."

"All of which the thieves disable before they get into the house," Colin told her.

"These thieves are tech savvy?" she asked.

He nodded, noticing that Heather seemed to be hanging on every word. "Looks that way."

"What are the names of the security companies?" Ellie asked.

He thought for a moment, recalling what was written on the reports. "Supreme Alarms."

"Just one name?" she asked. "Aren't there any other companies?"

He paused to mentally review the reports he'd read. "I don't think so."

"Maybe you should find out if the company recently fired anyone in the last few months. One of them might be looking for revenge. Disgruntled employees like to find a way to get back at their employers for firing them. This sounds like a perfect way to do it to me."

He grinned at her. "You are a very handy person to have around. We investigated the employees currently working for the company. We *didn't* look into any former employees," he admitted. "Don't know why I didn't think of this myself."

"See, Uncle Colin?" Heather spoke up. "Told you she was great."

Ellie quickly glossed over the compliment. "You would have thought of that," she assured him. "I just beat you to it because I love reading mystery thrillers," she told the detective.

Colin kept a straight face as he said, "Either that or you think like a thief."

"There's that, too," she agreed in the same deadpan voice.

"No, you're not a thief," Heather piped up.

"Ellie's just kidding," Colin told his niece. "In any case, I'm going to head down to the Supreme Alert main office in the morning, see if I can get a list of terminated employees."

She didn't know why she suddenly felt the need to warn him, but she did. "Be careful."

"Always," he assured her. "Except when it comes to the dog," Colin said, looking down. Apparently, Pancakes had decided to work on the leg of the chair he was sitting on. Bending over, he urged the dog away, bribing her with a piece of meat. "What did you say the name of that spray was?" he asked Ellie when he straightened up.

He knew she'd told him about it, but he'd put it out of his mind at the time. He was beginning to think that maybe he shouldn't have.

"Bitter apple," she repeated.

"I'm buying a gallon of it first thing in the morning," he vowed.

"Good thinking," she agreed as Heather dutifully drew the puppy away, offering her a chew toy instead. Pancakes took the bait.

Chapter Thirteen

"What are you doing on Thanksgiving?"

The question, asked by Colin, came seemingly out of the blue after dinner one evening.

Ellie was helping him load the dishwasher and the question caught her completely by surprise. She didn't answer him immediately. Instead, she glanced at the calendar Colin had hung up on the wall next to the sink.

The holiday had just crept up on her this year. It seemed like one day Thanksgiving was over a month away, the next it was almost upon her. Four days away to be exact.

Realizing that Colin was still waiting for some kind of an answer, Ellie shrugged. "Same thing I usually do. I'm working." What she left out was that she'd asked to be working on that day.

"Can't you get out of it?" he asked, rinsing off the casserole dish before tucking it in on the top rack. "You have seniority. After all, you've been there a few years now, right?"

Handing him the dishwashing liquid, Ellie looked at him. "Have you been reading my studio bio?" she asked, doing her best to sound lighthearted rather than defensive.

If Colin detected a slight edge in her voice, he gave no indication.

"I'm a detective—comes with the territory. So, can you get out of working?" he asked, then added, "I've got the day off."

Ellie pressed her lips together. Thanksgiving had always been rather special to her. Brett had proposed to her on Thanksgiving Day. Moreover, the Thanksgivings that came after that, if they'd been apart because he was overseas on a tour of duty, they still managed to spend the holiday "together," thanks to Skype.

Because of the time differences involved, sometimes she had to get up at three in the morning, and sometimes the first chance he had to talk to her was far into the wee hours at night. The inconvenience didn't matter. It was well worth it to her.

After she'd lost Brett, the thought of facing the holiday alone—even at her mother's house, and her mother always had a houseful of friends coming over—was just too painful for her to contemplate.

But this year, things had changed without her being fully aware of the metamorphosis. This year, she'd somehow gotten pulled into this do-it-yourself family comprised of Colin and his niece—and the dog—and she had to admit that she did like it. This was what she'd envisioned her life to be if she and Brett had had a child.

"Well, I guess that I could talk to the program manager," Ellie said evasively. "I'm not making any promises, but maybe…" She deliberately let her voice trail off.

Colin closed the dishwasher and started the washing process.

"Good," he said as if it was already a done deal. "Because I know that Heather would love to have you join us." Hoping to sweeten the deal, he told her, "I was thinking of going to The Five Crowns and I have to call in a reservation, the earlier, the better."

Ellie stared at him. "A restaurant?" she said in disbelief. "Seriously?"

Why was she looking at him as if he'd just assumed the role of the village idiot? "Yes, what's wrong with that?"

Ellie started to enumerate why his thinking was so wrong. "Number one, good luck with getting a reservation at this late date."

"Late date?" he challenged. "It's still five days away."

"Four," she corrected. "And even if you could get a reservation, which is doubtful, you don't go to a restaurant for Thanksgiving." How could he even *think* that was acceptable?

Maybe she hadn't made the connection between all the takeout menus tacked up on his refrigerator and the fact that he'd never invited her to a home-cooked meal that *he* had made.

"You do if your cooking skills are limited to scrambled eggs and toast—usually burnt," he added.

"Well, mine aren't and it's important that Heather has a home-cooked Thanksgiving meal." It was happening again. She was getting pulled further in by volunteering to cook Thanksgiving dinner. Moreover, if she was being honest with herself, she hadn't made the offer against her will. "Okay," she said, "if I can clear the day with my program manager at the station, I'll make the turkey."

"I don't want to put you out." His protest was at odds with the broad smile on his face.

Her eyes met his. "Sure you do, but it's understandable, given the situation." At least her mother would be overjoyed that she was doing this, she couldn't help thinking. "I'm putting you on notice, by the way."

"About?" he asked, not quite sure what he was bracing himself for.

There wasn't a thing in his refrigerator or pantry she could work with—other than margarine. "If I get the go-ahead from the program manager, you and I and Heather are going food shopping."

"You're the boss," he told her, relieved that *this* was her condition and not something else.

"Right," she mocked.

She wasn't the boss in this situation, Ellie thought. If anything, she was just along for the ride. But somehow, she couldn't summon any resentment or indignation over the very gentle way she'd been manipulated. That in itself spoke volumes, but she chose not to explore that now.

In his sixth decade, Marty Stern was a thin, wiry man who was very good at his job. He always appeared to be moving, juggling a myriad of tasks, usually at the same time, and remarkably, keeping them all straight. His gift was that he always remained on top of everything that came under the heading of his job.

His approval wasn't easily won, but once it was, that person had it for life. He had a fondness for Ellie. In all the time she'd been with the station, she had never once questioned any assignment he had given her, any place he had sent her.

So when she'd knocked on his door the following morning and asked for a few minutes of his time, he had beckoned her in and heard her out.

When she'd finished, he had to admit to himself that she'd surprised him.

"Seriously?" he asked her, looking at her over his steepled thin fingers. "You want Thanksgiving off?" Given what he knew, he hadn't expected this.

"Yes. But if it puts you in a bind—" she began, about to rescind her request. She'd never been one who caused problems and maybe this had been a bad idea.

"No," Marty told her, cutting her off, "actually, I can get someone to cover your spot. I just thought you said you *wanted* to work on Thanksgiving."

"I did say that," she confirmed. "But something came up."

"A good something?" Marty asked, eyeing her closely.

"A different something."

Would she jinx it by saying yes? She wasn't normally superstitious but in the last couple of years, she had lost track of exactly what "normal" was. Ellie decided to take the safe route.

"Okay," he laughed drily, "I'll accept that. You've

got the day off. Lord knows you've earned it," he told her. "Now go get me something on that bear sighting down in Mission Viejo. Preferably some footage," he said, sending her off.

"You've got it." It was as good as a promise. She planned to do her very best.

Ellie had no sooner gotten into the news van with Jerry and started down the Santa Ana Freeway than she felt her phone vibrate.

Pulling it out of her pocket, she saw that it wasn't a call coming in but a text. She recognized the number. Colin was sending her a text.

Any word yet?

Smiling to herself, Ellie texted back, Got the day off.

The moment she sent it out, she received another text in response.

Great!

She was tempted to text back an inquiry as to whether he was experiencing a slow day, allowing him time to text, but she refrained. Instead, she put her phone away. When she looked up, she saw that Jerry was watching her.

"Never saw you texting before. Something I should know?" Her cameraman was grinning from ear to ear, as if he already had the answer to his question.

Ellie pointed to his front windshield. "Yes, you

should know that more accidents happen when you take your eyes off the road—so watch the road."

If anything, his grin got wider. There was no denying that he was very amused by all this.

"Anything else I should know?" he teased.

Ellie sighed as she sank back in her seat. "Just that your wife's a saint for putting up with you."

Threading his way onto the freeway, he paused until they merged into the left lane. "Speaking of wife, you know that our usual invitation to join us for Thanksgiving still stands if you decide to change your mind about working."

She realized that he didn't know yet. She didn't want to get into it, but then, she didn't want him being the last to know, either.

"Sorry, I've got plans," she told him, hoping that was the end of it.

It was obvious that her answer surprised him. "'Plan' plans?" Jerry asked keenly, making it sound like some sort of secret undertaking.

"Just drive, Jerry," she ordered.

His curiosity aroused, he knew better than to prod her. She'd tell him when she was ready. "Good for you, Ellie."

"Jerry—" There was a warning note in her voice as she said his name.

"I'm driving, I'm driving," he answered, backing off even more.

But she noted that he was still grinning. And, in a way, she supposed that she was, too.

"How about this one?" Colin asked two evenings later when they finally found the time to go shopping.

He was holding up a twenty-five-pound frozen turkey for her approval. Because of both their schedules, this was the first opportunity that they had to go to the supermarket together.

Ellie supposed that it would have probably been a lot quicker for her to just go alone, but she wanted to include Heather in the safari and she knew that the girl would want her uncle to come, as well, which was how they all came to be in the well-stocked chain supermarket at seven thirty in the evening, shopping for Thanksgiving.

Despite it being two days away from Thanksgiving, there was no shortage of turkeys to choose from.

"That depends on whether you want to be eating turkey leftovers for the next week and a half or not. There'll just be three of us," she reminded him. "A ten- to twelve-pound turkey will do."

"Okay." Colin put the turkey back in the open freezer where the store had placed most of their stock of birds and searched until he found one the size that she'd suggested. Picking it up, he eyed it skeptically. "Really? It looks puny."

"I'm not telling you *not* to get the larger one," she told him. "But just remember that there's just so much you can do with leftover turkey."

"I love turkey sandwiches," Heather spoke up. There was more than a trace of nostalgia in her voice as she said, "Mom would put them in my lunch all week."

The argument was settled in Colin's mind.

"A bigger bird it is," he announced, returning the smaller specimen and taking one that weighed in at sixteen pounds. In his mind, it was the perfect compromise. "What's next?"

"We need to make stuffing," Ellie said.

Colin thought for a minute. He didn't frequent grocery stores all that often. "I think I saw the boxes in the next aisle," he told her.

Ellie stopped him before he could turn on his heel. "We're not going to eat stuffing that came in a box."

"We're not?" Colin turned around to face her. "Are these rules written down someplace?" he asked. His personal rule of thumb was always the simpler, the better.

"Just work with me," Ellie told him, then rattled off the ingredients for the stuffing that her mother always made. She'd never met anyone who didn't like it. "Okay, we're going to need two packages of hot sausages, one package of medium-hot sausage, a pound of hard salami, several cans of chicken broth, some celery and two large loaves of white bread."

"All that for stuffing?" Colin asked doubtfully.

"Only if you want to do it right," she answered.

"Well, that puts me in my place," Colin replied obligingly.

Once they'd located all the ingredients she needed and placed them in the cart, Ellie turned toward Heather. "You get to pick the vegetables and the dessert."

Happy to contribute, Heather said, "That's easy. My mom always made mashed potatoes and corn on the cob. Oh, and gravy," she added.

"And for dessert?" Ellie coaxed.

That drew an even bigger smile from the girl.

"Pumpkin pie," Heather said as if she could all but taste it.

"See?" Ellie said to Colin, who was on the other side of the cart—Heather insisted on being the one to push it. She gestured to the contents in the cart. "Now *that's* a Thanksgiving dinner."

"It still has to be cooked," Colin pointed out. "That's where the real work comes in."

"Heather and I will handle it," Ellie said, looking at the girl. "Won't we?"

Heather looked as if she was willing to get started the second they got home. "You bet."

It did Colin's heart good to hear his niece sounding so happy. And he knew that he owed it, at least in part, to Ellie. The woman was becoming very precious to him, he thought.

Because the turkey weighed in at a little over sixteen pounds, it was going to need to be in the oven for four hours after it was cleaned and draped with cheesecloth, the latter properly doused with melted butter. In addition, the stuffing needed be made before that. Between toasting the bread and cutting each slice into tiny pieces, plus frying the sausages to get rid of any excess fat, Ellie knew that would take her another hour. By her calculations, she needed to get started by ten, which meant day off or not, she had to get up a lot earlier.

Even so, she was going to be busy for most of that morning. She was trying to time everything down to the minute so that all of her time was taken up with preparing the dinner. She deliberately didn't want to give herself any time to think. Thinking only made her dwell on the past—and remember what she didn't have anymore.

"Not the time for it now," she sternly told her reflection in the wardrobe mirror when she caught herself mentally drifting for a moment. "It's not about you. There's a little girl counting on you to make today special."

Heather's loss was fresher than her own and she wouldn't forgive herself if she didn't do everything she could to make this Thanksgiving a good one for the little girl.

In her heart, Ellie knew that her husband would have wanted her to do this. He would have wanted her to move on because he was that sort of a selfless person. He'd always told her that he wanted her to be happy and if anything ever happened to him, he wanted her to find someone to love.

Because you've got so much love in you, Ellie. You can't keep it all bottled up—you have to find someone to share it with.

He'd made these declarations when he was being deployed, thinking that he might die fighting for his country. Neither one of them had ever dreamed that he would meet his end stateside, not fighting for his country but defending an unarmed young couple.

"I'm trying, Brett," she murmured as she got dressed. "But you've got to help me. I can't do this alone."

And then she looked at her watch. It was after nine. She should have left fifteen minutes ago. She'd set a schedule for herself in her head, the way she did every day no matter what she was doing. It kept her organized.

It also kept her from thinking too much. And that was the way she liked it. Right now all she wanted to focus on was making a good Thanksgiving dinner. After that, she told herself, she'd focus on something else.

Her mother had told her shortly after Brett's death that the way to get through the oppressive pain and the horrific grief was to take one step at a time.

Just one step at a time, Elliana. You'll be surprised how those steps add up—and where they lead to.

Her mother had said that recalling her grief when her own husband had died.

Ellie had never hoped her mother was right as much as she did today.

Chapter Fourteen

It seemed that the very second Ellie knocked on the door, it swung open. Colin was in the doorway, a broad smile on his face.

"Wow, if I didn't know any better, I would have said you were standing right behind the door," Ellie said as she walked in.

"I was," he told her, closing the door behind her. When she looked at him quizzically, he said, "Heather alerted me. She'd been at the window watching for you for the last hour." He nodded toward the dog that was trying to snag her attention. "I don't know who's been jumping around more, Heather or Pancakes."

"Well, it's nice to be greeted with this much enthusiasm," Ellie said, shifting the grocery bags she was carrying so she could give Heather a quick hug.

Not wanting to leave her out, she petted the bouncing dog. The latter tried to catch hold of her sleeve with her teeth, an act Ellie managed to deftly avoid.

His niece and the dog weren't the only ones looking forward to her arrival, but Colin deliberately refrained from saying anything because he didn't want to send her running back to the shelter of her car. He sensed that she was still skittish and he approached Ellie with caution.

Instead, he nodded at what she'd brought in. "What's in the grocery bags? I thought we got everything for today."

After setting the bags down on the kitchen counter, Ellie proceeded to unpack them. "These are just a few miscellaneous things I forgot to pick up during our shopping trip the other night."

Colin grabbed the item that was closest to him. "Parmesan cheese?" he questioned.

"That's for the mashed potatoes," she explained, then offered, "Do you want me to go over what everything else is for?"

"No, I'll learn as we go along," Colin answered, a bemused smile on his face.

Ellie returned one in kind. "See, you're learning already." Turning to Heather, she said, "Okay, assistant, let's get to work, shall we?"

"What can I do?" Colin asked.

Ellie turned around to regard him for a moment. "How are you at peeling potatoes?"

"You're giving me KP duty?" he asked with less than enthusiasm over the prospect.

"Extremely important KP duty," Ellie emphasized. She gestured toward the bag he had out on the counter. "We've got five pounds of potatoes that need peeling."

With a resigned shrug, he said, "I guess I can't ruin that."

Ellie made no effort to hide her amusement. "Not unless you cut off one of your fingers."

"Thanks for the vote of confidence," Colin pretended to grumble.

Ellie spread her hands wide, feigning innocence. "Hey, you were the one who said you didn't exactly shine in the kitchen."

He inclined his head as if to give her the round. He took out a knife from the last drawer on the right hand side. "You want all of them peeled?"

"Peeled and cut up into very small pieces." When he seemed confused, she explained, "They cook faster that way."

Nodding, he slid open the bag, allowing him to take the potatoes out. "Anything else?"

She was already slicing open the individual sausages, getting them ready to be put in the frying pan. "When you finish that, I need five celery stalks finely diced." She turned her attention to his niece, who was impatiently shifting from foot to foot. "Heather, your job is to toast the bread. We're going to need all the slices from both loaves."

"You got it," Heather told her happily, throwing herself into the task.

The rest of the morning was spent doing all the things that were involved in preparing a proper Thanksgiving meal. To a casual observer, it would look like just barely organized chaos, with Pancakes weaving in and out between all of them, continuously foraging for any bit of food that had been dropped on the floor. The only time the dog stopped foraging was when she found something. At that point, she disposed of it at lightning speed.

And then went back to foraging.

There seemed to be no downtime, not even when the turkey was finally basted, draped and in the oven, baking. At that point, Ellie turned her attention to making the pumpkin pie and the rolls she'd decided to add at the last minute.

Heather appeared to be in heaven and Colin, although not in heaven, was enjoying seeing Heather so involved and so content. He knew he had Ellie to thank for that.

"You realize that you were on your feet the entire time?" Colin asked when they finally sat down to eat dinner hours later. "From the minute you walked in to just now, when I finally got you to sit down to eat with us?" For a second there, he'd been afraid that she was bent on cleaning up, leaving Heather and him to eat while she tidied.

"It's no different than when I'm out on assignment," she answered. "Just a little hotter," she added, indicating the stove. He had a relatively small kitchen, so the heat was difficult to avoid and it was an unusually warm Thanksgiving, even for Southern California. "Except when they send me out of state to cover a story smack in the middle of a heat wave," she added as a postscript.

"I take it you don't believe in complaining," he said to her.

Ellie shrugged. "What good would it do?" She watched Colin and his niece, looking from one to the other, waiting for some sort of a reaction. They'd both started eating. "Well?" she finally asked. "How is it?"

Colin stared at her, pretending to consider her question for a moment before saying, "Oh, well, maybe it's a little undercooked."

"What?" Ellie cried, surprised as well as mystified. "But I timed it and the skin is just crisp enough—" She stopped abruptly because Colin had started laughing.

"I'm sorry—I'm just kidding. This is probably the best turkey I've ever had. Ow!" he cried when Ellie took a swipe at his arm. He gave her what he assumed might pass for a reproving look. "You realize that I could take you in for assaulting an officer of the law, right?" he told her.

Ellie raised her chin. "You'd have to catch me first."

"Don't tempt me," Colin told her, the expression in his eyes saying things that he didn't—or couldn't at the moment.

"He's just kidding, Ellie," Heather assured her, eating merrily. "And this is really, really good."

Ellie smiled at her fondly. "And you know why?"

Heather swallowed, then answered, "'Cause of all those things you put in?"

Ellie nodded. "Yes, but mainly because we all worked together to make it. Things always taste better when you make them yourself," she told the girl with feeling.

"Obviously, I'm going to have to make you breakfast someday," Colin told her with a laugh.

For just a second, their eyes met and Ellie felt a shiver go down her spine, the kind a person felt in anticipation of something that hadn't been experienced yet. He was talking about making her breakfast. Did he mean after they spent the night together, or was that an entirely innocent comment on his part?

You're doing it again. You're overthinking things. Take what he said at face value and nothing more.

Ellie glanced away. Looking into his eyes did unsettling things to her.

"Okay," she told him, smiling even when he went on to describe the ingredients that went into his perfect breakfast, items that had no business on the same plate. Even so, she was relieved that the dinner was a success. She began to relax and started to actually taste—and enjoy—what she had prepared.

After dinner and dessert had been eaten and savored, at Heather's behest, the three of them sat down and watched the tail end of the second football game on TV that day.

"This your idea?" she asked Colin as they settled on the sofa to watch.

He shook his head. "Not guilty. This is strictly Heather's idea," he said, nodding at his niece.

Heather was nestled between them, her attention riveted on the TV monitor. At first Heather thought the girl hadn't heard them, but then, still watching, she said, "My dad always liked to watch the games on Thanksgiving. Mom said we had to keep him company because he loved watching the games almost as much as he loved us." For just a second, she spared Ellie a glance. "It makes me feel closer to them watching the game now."

Moved, Ellie gave her a hug. She could totally relate to the need to bond across time and space.

"I've just got one question," she told Heather. "Who's playing?"

With a delighted air of superiority, Heather answered her question, throwing in both teams' stats as an added bonus.

"So what'd you think of it?" Ellie asked the little girl when the game was finally over almost two hours later.

When she received no answer, she was about to repeat her question, then stopped. Leaning in closer, she took another look and then smiled. Raising her head again, she turned toward Colin.

"Don't look now, but your little football fan is fast asleep."

"I know," he told her. He'd watched the rest of the game not because he particularly cared about the outcome but because he just liked sitting with them like this. There was something so right about it and he hadn't wanted to disturb the scene. "We lost her shortly after the third quarter started."

After getting up so as not to wake up Heather, he gently eased his niece off the sofa and into his arms. Asleep, she looked even younger than she was. "I'll just put her to bed."

Ellie was on her feet. "Need any help?"

"No," he whispered, "I'm just going to lay her down and cover her with a blanket. She's a light sleeper. If I do anything else, even take off her shoes, I'm liable to wake her up and then she'll be up for hours again. I've learned from experience that a forty-five-minute nap can really power her up. She's better off if I just let her sleep in her clothes. I'll be right back," he promised, turning away.

"Don't trip on the dog," Ellie warned in a stage whisper. Pancakes was sprawled out near the sofa, directly in his path. "Apparently, football puts her to sleep, too."

"Maybe we're onto something," Colin said with a laugh just before he made his way out of the room with Heather in his arms.

When he returned several minutes later, the TV was still on, but Ellie was no longer on the sofa or even in the room.

Colin looked around. He half expected her to be getting her things together to go home.

He knew that she'd spent almost an entire day with them, but even so, he didn't really want her to leave just yet. He liked her company, liked doing simple, ordinary things with this woman who regularly found her way into everyone's home for four or five minutes at a time.

This was different from that.

He wasn't really certain just what was going on, because he'd never felt quite like this before, never wanted to have a woman around to this extent.

But then, this wasn't just a woman; this was a unique, special woman. He couldn't help wondering what Ellie would say if he told her that.

Probably take off faster. He had to tread carefully if he wanted this—whatever "this" was—to progress.

Since she hadn't said anything about leaving, there was only one other place she could be. Ellie had to be in the kitchen, cleaning up. The dishes had previously been left where they were because of the football game. He'd just naturally assumed that he'd tackle them in the morning.

"You don't have to do that," he told Ellie, walking into the room.

She shrugged as if this was no big deal. "It's part of the process. First you cook, then you eat and then you clean up." She spared him a quick glance over her shoulder. "You really don't want to have to face this mess in the morning," she told him knowingly. "Besides, I'm almost done."

"But you're not loading the dishwasher," Colin observed. There were soap bubbles rising from a filled sink. He assumed the dishes were in there. "You're washing them."

"Sometimes," she said, keeping her back to Colin, "sinking your hands into a sink full of suds is therapeutic." And she did just that.

He came up behind her. "Is it working for you?" he asked kindly.

She didn't answer his question. Instead, she told him, "I enjoyed today. I think Heather did, too."

"Oh, I know she did," he declared with certainty. And then he told her, "Thank you."

She deflected his thanks. "I really didn't do anything. I just made a turkey."

Colin suppressed a sigh. "Do you *ever* just take a compliment?"

"Sure," she answered a bit too quickly. "If I deserve it."

"Well, there is no 'if' here," he said. "You did a really good thing and you made my niece very happy." She was still keeping her back to him and he found that a little strange. Something wasn't quite right here, he thought. "Will you just turn around from the sink and let me thank you?"

When she slowly turned around, Colin saw why she'd kept her face averted. Something squeezed his heart. "You're crying."

She knew she couldn't deny it, but she didn't want him questioning her about it.

"I get sentimental over soapsuds," she said, quickly wiping away the tear tracks from her cheeks with the back of her hand. That only made the situation worse because her hand was wet.

Colin took out his handkerchief, and ever so carefully, he wiped her cheeks. "Try again," he told her softly.

Ellie tried to turn away, shrugging off his concern, even though he'd all but melted her just now. "I'm fine," she insisted.

But he wasn't going to be put off. Colin took her into his arms.

"No, you're not," he told her. "Maybe if you talk about it—"

"No, no talking," she protested, shaking her head. "No—"

And then something seemed to just break apart inside her. She'd started by pulling away, and somehow, inexplicably, she wound up even closer to him than before. So close that the next moment, her resolve cracked. Ellie gave in to the overwhelming desire she felt to fill the emptiness inside her.

In a blinding flash, she was kissing him. Kissing him because the first time they'd kissed, she'd felt that old, familiar feeling she'd missed so much.

It was like a homecoming.

The kiss blossomed, catching her up in the feeling, reminding her how wondrous it could all be.

She wanted Colin to make her forget what she'd lost. She wanted him to make her forget the pain she couldn't seem to outrun no matter how fast she moved.

The pain that seemed to fade only when he was kissing her.

With superhuman effort, he gently pushed her away from him. "Ellie, wait." Stunned, Colin struggled to rein in his own almost overpowering reaction, his own fierce desire to let all this progress down its natural path.

He was *not* about to take advantage of Ellie's vulnerability unless and until she could really convince him that this was what she unquestionably wanted.

She blinked, trying to focus. Her orientation was askew. "Why?"

"Don't get the wrong idea," he warned. "I'd like nothing better than to have this go where I think it's going. But I'm not going to let that happen unless I think that you really want this, too. That you're not just doing it because things have gotten out of hand."

Ellie stared at him, her mind not fully processing what was going on. "You're going to make me beg?"

"No, not beg," he said quickly. "Just convince me." It was almost a plea on his part.

The words were finally penetrating. She knew she should just back off, go home before she did something she would regret.

But going home might just be the thing that she *would* regret. "Wow, are you asking for this in writing?"

He couldn't help himself. He was framing her face

with his hands, his eyes communing with hers. "No, but I want you to be really, really sure."

Were men actually this good? Was he worried about her? She felt herself being drawn even closer to him. "I didn't realize you were a Boy Scout."

"No, not a Boy Scout," he assured Ellie. "Just a man who really doesn't want you to feel like you've made a mistake in the morning."

Damn, that clinched it. Every inch of her just wanted him to hold her. To make love to her and make her feel that everything would be all right again, the way it once was.

"Shut up, Benteen," she ordered. "Shut up and kiss me."

Not waiting for him to comply, she brought her mouth up to his again. And then over and over again, effectively blowing his resolve into the same little pieces that hers had become.

Weakening, Colin tried just one more time.

"Ellie—"

He got no further. He gave in to her. He gave in to himself. The next moment, Colin was kissing her back, kissing her the way he'd wanted to kiss her these last few weeks.

Kissing her the way he'd never kissed another woman, because he'd never felt about another woman the way he did about her.

Chapter Fifteen

"It's all right," Ellie whispered, thinking Colin still expected her to change her mind when he pulled back again.

"It's more than all right," he answered, referring to the kiss that had just spun through his system, leaving him wanting more. "But not out here."

There was a time when he would have just gone with the desire pulsating through him, making love on any surface that was available. It was the act that was important, as well as the woman of the moment, not the location.

But all that had been in a life that occurred BH— Before Heather. These days, no matter what his feelings were about anything else and no matter how urgent they seemed, his niece and her welfare always had priority. That included anything that she might encounter or see that could in turn affect her in an adverse way.

"Heather might come out and find us," he explained to Ellie. "This is *not* the way I want her to learn about the facts of life."

Ellie smiled, his thoughtfulness regarding his niece really touching her. "She's ten. I'm sure she already knows. Girls grow up a lot faster these days."

Colin groaned, anticipating what he might have to deal with down the line—sooner than later. "Oh Lord, I hope not." The next moment, he tabled that discussion by sweeping Ellie into his arms.

"What are you doing?" she laughed, steadying herself by anchoring her arms around his neck.

"Can't you tell?" he deadpanned. "I'm having my way with you." Then, before she could ask him anything else, Colin covered her lips with his own, all the while carrying her to his bedroom.

He'd left his bedroom door opened. He made his way in now, then pushed the door closed with his elbow. After setting her down on the floor, he flipped the lock to ensure that Heather couldn't just walk in on them, accidentally advancing her education further tonight in ways none of them wanted.

Once that was out of the way, he gathered Ellie to him, dissolving any resistance, any second thoughts she might still be harboring about his intent by kissing her over and over. Each kiss was more passionate, more burning, than the last until the whole room seemed to be enveloped in a circle of heat—and getting hotter by the second.

It had been more than two years since she'd known the touch of a man's hand. More than two years since she'd felt this rush of desire, of heated anticipation coursing though her veins. Suddenly, she was a prisoner of her own yearning, a yearning that was all but pleading to be satisfied.

Ellie stifled a moan as she felt his fingers working apart the buttons, one at a time, that ran down the front of her sweater. She felt her skin heating beneath his fingers. He coaxed the garment off her shoulders, then tossed it aside. Her slacks were next. He undid the button at the top, then slowly slid down the zipper with his fingertip. Ellie shivered, waiting.

She felt the material being eased down along her hips even as his lips were slowly branding her mouth, her throat, then moving down to the swell of her breasts.

Her own restraint shredded apart. Ellie began to urgently undo his pants, his shirt, desperate to get all the barriers out of her way so she could run her hands along his body, could feel his taut, naked skin against hers.

Finally, there was nothing left between them except red-hot desire. Clothing dispensed with, they merged in an embrace, melding themselves one against the other, seeking to pleasure each other, seeking to absorb the pleasures they rendered to each other so effortlessly.

Within seconds, they wound up on Colin's bed, rolling about on the king-size comforter, their limbs entwined as their anticipation rose to new, almost sizzling heights that threatened to consume them both.

His arms were strong as they enclosed around her, making her feel as if she had found a new haven, somewhere where nothing could ever harm her, where nothing could find her. She gave herself up to the feelings, to the man who created them within her, stunned that this was actually happening.

She'd given up hope of ever feeling this way again because she'd deliberately banished all feelings for fear of the pain that loomed in their wake—and yet here she was, experiencing all that and more.

She was thrilled, even as fear still hovered along the outer perimeter of her consciousness.

Her heart pounding, Ellie felt him press her back against the bed, his body just over hers. But instead of doing what she expected, instead of uniting with her body then and there, Colin slowly moved down along her body, covering every inch he came in contact with in moist, open-mouth, hot kisses.

Thorough, he left no part of her untouched, beginning with her mouth, moving down to her chin, then to her throat. He continued, making his way down along her breasts, first one, then the other, his tongue artfully teasing each tip before forging an intricate trail down along her belly, which quivered as he slid his tongue along the area.

His warm breath made her tremble in agonizing eagerness as he made his way down farther and farther until he was at her inner core, his tongue moving at a maddeningly slow pace, going back and forth— creating ripening, exploding peaks within her.

Ellie grabbed fistfuls of his comforter, arching her back off his bed, first moving with and then away from the exquisite sensation, trying to absorb as much as she could without crying out.

And then the ultimate climax seized her and she scrambled, arching even higher, wanting to go on savoring forever what she was feeling—even as she knew that it was an impossibility.

The intensity waned. Spent, Ellie fell back on the bed, her eyes widening in exhausted amazement as she looked at him.

She expected that would be all.

She expected wrong.

The next moment, Colin moved his body up over hers, ready to become one with her. He'd held back for as long as humanly possible, held back because he wanted her to be ready, wanted the foreplay to show her that he was mindful of her needs, not just his own.

But he couldn't hold back his own need for her even a microsecond longer.

Linking his hands with hers, Colin threaded their fingers together and was more than ready to complete the union.

"Open your eyes, Ellie," he whispered against her ear, then lifted his head as he told her, "Look at me."

When she did, he entered her and then the dance began, a dance as old as time, as fresh as tomorrow—as unique as they were to one another.

The tempo was slow at first, but then the music in their heads increased. They went faster, then faster still, daring one another to reach that golden pinnacle, racing to get there, to bring the other along.

They did it together.

Colin squeezed her hands as the moment found them, culminating in a burst of fireworks before slowly fading into the sky of the world they had created together.

Ellie hung on to the euphoria for as long as she could until there was nothing more to hang on to. She felt the tension leave his body, felt him roll off hers. To her surprise, he didn't get up, nor did he turn over on his side and fall asleep. Instead, he gathered her to him as if she was something precious, something he cherished that he wanted to hold on to.

Ellie moved her head onto his chest. She became aware of Colin's heart beating beneath her cheek. She couldn't explain why that comforted her, but it did. And that was enough for now.

After a while—she wasn't sure just how long— he raised his head to look at her, asking, "Are you all right?"

The question made her smile. "I'll let you know when I come back to earth."

"Fair enough," he said, inclining his head, then adding, "I just wanted to make sure I didn't hurt you."

Hurt her? She laughed softly to herself. "You didn't exactly toss me off a building."

"There are a lot of ways a person can get hurt," Colin pointed out gently.

Ellie turned her body to his, feeling a flicker of desire returning. The lights were off in his room but there was a full moon out and his window was right in its path, allowing its light to come in.

He really cared, she realized. Something tugged at her heart. Ordinarily, that would have been an urgent warning sign, a signal for her to turn tail and run. But she was far too spent to run and far too naked to get very far. She remained where she was, where she wanted to be.

Ellie touched his face, her fingers skimming along Colin's cheek. A five-o'clock shade had already begun encroaching on his face. He had a kind face, she thought, and even as glimmers of fear raised their head, she was happy.

To show him how she felt, because the words were just not coming, Ellie raised her head ever so slightly and brushed her lips against his.

And then she did it again, because once was not enough.

And before she knew it, they were doing it all over again, making love as if the first time hadn't happened. As if they each needed to get their fill of one another again. Because once was not enough.

She knew she should be leaving.

Ellie promised herself that the second he was asleep, she was going to slip out of bed, gather her clothes to her and get dressed in the bathroom so she didn't wake him, then leave.

That was her plan.

But she fell asleep before Colin did, so she never got to execute her plan the way she wanted to.

And when she did wake up, with hints of sunlight beginning to tiptoe through the bedroom, the thought of making an escape somehow just wasn't appealing. So when she finally slipped out of his bed and padded her way to the bathroom to get dressed, she did so with the intention of making breakfast.

Somehow, it only seemed right to her.

Ellie crept as soundlessly as she could through his bedroom. Coming to the door, she worked the lock slowly, moving it by fractions of an inch until she had it in the unlocked position. When she finally had it unlocked, she eased the door opened, looking carefully from one side to the other. The last thing she wanted to do was run into Heather as she was leaving her uncle's bedroom.

Yes, she thought, girls knew a few more things at ten than she had at that age, but she didn't want to put that to the test, just in case Heather was still as sweetly innocent as she looked.

Relieved when she saw that the door to Heather's room was still closed, Ellie let out the breath she'd been holding and quickly made her way into the kitchen.

Once she was there, breakfast got under way.

She moved as fast as she could without making any noise. She was so intent on being silent that she didn't hear him until he was directly behind her.

"Morning, beautiful," Colin said, threading his arms around her waist from behind and hugging her to him.

Ellie jumped, stifling what amounted to a yelp.

"Hey, easy, now—it's me. Who did you think it was?" he asked her, laughing.

Spatula in hand, she turned around to face him, her heart still hammering wildly in her chest. It felt as if it was about to break out of her rib cage at any moment.

"I thought you were still in bed," she cried. It sounded almost like an accusation.

"I was, until I saw that it was empty. I thought maybe you'd taken off," he confessed, then added with an approving smile, "This is a much nicer surprise." He meant finding her in the kitchen. Then he looked around, taking in the broader picture. "What are you doing?"

"What does it look like?" she replied. "I'm making breakfast."

"I could have made breakfast for us," he told her. It seemed only right after she'd spent half of yesterday cooking for Heather and him. It seemed even more so since she'd given him an unimaginable night that he wasn't going to ever forget.

But Ellie shook her head, vetoing the suggestion. "After the way you described it, I thought we'd be better off if I made breakfast." Mischief glinted in her eyes as she told him, "I have no desire to spend the day after Thanksgiving in the emergency room, having my stomach pumped."

"It's not that bad," he protested. And then he shrugged, conceding the possible validity of what she'd said. "But it's not all that good, either."

Ellie nodded, sliding the eggs she'd just made onto a plate and then quickly taking out two slices of toast from the toaster. She buttered them quickly before cutting the slices in half and putting them on either side of the eggs.

"I like a man who knows his shortcomings," she told him.

He grinned, fighting the urge to forget about breakfast and just take her back to his bed. "As long as that word doesn't apply to last night."

"No," she assured him with feeling, "definitely not to last night." Changing the topic before she weakened, she said, "I've got coffee." Ellie indicated the coffee-maker over on the far corner of the counter.

"I'm more interested in something else you have," he told her, the corners of his mouth curving in a wicked smile.

"This morning is PG rated," she reminded him, nodding toward the hall beyond the kitchen.

The next moment, Heather came in, looking as if she hadn't fully woken up yet.

"That smells good," she said, taking a deep breath.

"Thank you—yours is coming up in a second," Ellie promised.

Heather's eyes narrowed as she looked at her, then down at herself before slanting a glance at her uncle. "How come you've got different clothes on?" she asked her uncle. "Ellie and I are wearing the same clothes we had on yesterday."

He was relieved that instead of questioning why Ellie was wearing the same clothes she'd had on yesterday, Heather had turned the question around, wondering why he was the odd man out.

"Well, um, I spilled some gravy on my shirt and decided to put on a complete change of clothes," Colin told his niece.

Her eyebrows drew even closer together as if she assessed what he'd just told her. "I didn't see any gravy on your shirt."

"That's because it happened seconds *after* you fell asleep," he said without missing a beat.

"Oh, okay." Both Colin and Ellie thought they were out of the woods—but then Heather looked at her and asked, "Did you sleep here last night, Ellie?"

Ellie wasn't comfortable with lies. Lies always led to complications. So instead, Ellie told her, "You have a very comfortable couch," hoping the little girl would just make the leap.

"I fall asleep on that all the time," Heather confided, pleased that they had something in common.

"Heather, don't forget to feed Pancakes," Colin spoke up, reminding his niece of her responsibility.

As she went to get the dog food, he whispered to Ellie, "I noticed you didn't answer her question."

"Not directly," Ellie agreed, whispering back. "It's called a nonanswer."

He wondered if she was putting him on notice. Should he anticipate nonanswers from her, as well? The next moment, he just let the thought pass.

Heather returned and placed the filled dog's bowl down on the floor. Pancakes immediately dived in and began to eat, making short work of her breakfast.

"And here's your breakfast," Ellie told her, putting her dish down on the table in the girl's usual place.

Taking her seat, Heather appeared ready to dig in.

"Those eggs look a lot better than the ones Uncle Colin makes," she observed. And then she realized that she'd hurt his feelings with her honest assessment. Crying "Oops," Heather covered her mouth.

"That's okay, kid," he said, absolving her of any guilt on his behalf. "They *are* better. Eat up."

With an exaggerated sigh of relief, Heather did as she was told.

Chapter Sixteen

She kept telling herself to back off, to leave before she became too entrenched, too complacent.

Too happy.

The longer she remained, the more she felt it was like mocking the gods, and in every Greek mythology story she'd read as a child, mocking the gods never ended well for the one who did the mocking. The gods always got their revenge.

The only problem with all these points Ellie kept raising in her mind and her pep talks to herself was that it was already too late. Too late because she was too entrenched, too complacent and too happy for words.

And yes, she was afraid, *really* afraid that it would fall apart on her, but she just couldn't force herself to leave, to end this once and for all.

Several times she'd even rehearsed the words to tell Colin: that their relationship had run its course, that it was all a big mistake on her part and that they should just stop now and go their separate ways, remaining friends.

But she didn't want to be his friend, not when being his lover was so much more fulfilling. Life had meaning again and she no longer spent the first few minutes of every morning trying to pull herself up out of an oppressive abyss.

Instead, she woke up smiling.

Besides, she couldn't end it. There wasn't just herself to think of in this relationship, she argued. She'd become incredibly fond of Heather. They had bonded over their mutual experience of losing someone—in Heather's case, two someones. She just couldn't hurt the girl by ending it with Colin and walking out of her life, too.

If she did walk out, there was no way they could visit with one another. Doing something like that, walking away from Colin, would leave the girl reeling and in the terrible position where Heather felt she had to choose sides. Hers would of course have to be with her uncle. Anything else wasn't feasible.

Any way Ellie looked at it, terminating her relationship with Colin only led to unhappiness and hopelessness.

Especially for her.

So she continued seeing Colin and thus seeing Heather, continued as if everything was all right and that deep down in the recess of her soul, she wasn't haunted by the specter of a very real fear.

A fear that was always there, in the background,

stuffed into a corner and hardly noticeable except in the right light.

So she tried not to pay attention to it and prayed that eventually, the fear would lessen or just go away altogether.

In the meantime, Ellie lost herself in the demands of her job. In her off hours, she joined forces with Colin. Christmas was swiftly approaching and he'd asked her to help him make this a memorable celebration for Heather. His goal was to keep his niece too busy to have any time to be sad.

"It's going to be rough for her," Colin speculated one evening as they sat on the couch together talking after Heather had gone to bed. "This is her first Christmas without her parents and I know it's got to be making her unhappy, but I want to do something special for her to get her mind off the pain of missing them."

Ellie looked at him and she could almost see the wheels in his head turning as he swiftly examined and then discarded ideas. And then his eyes seemed to light up.

"Maybe I'll take some time off and we'll go to Disney World for a week," he said, turning toward Ellie and becoming more enthusiastic the more he thought about the idea.

She could see how that could be a good distraction for the ten-year-old, but there was a problem.

"It's a great idea, but I can't come with you. I can't take off for a week," she told him honestly. The holidays usually meant more work, not less. "The best I can do is get Christmas Eve and Christmas Day off."

Colin was nothing if not flexible. He was already

coming up with a plan B. "Okay, no Disney World. We'll do Disneyland, instead."

Ellie shook her head. There was a problem with that, too. "Disneyland is closed on Christmas," she pointed out.

"Closed? You're sure?" he questioned, momentarily disheartened.

"I'm afraid so."

Regrouping, Colin restructured his plan. What mattered here was some sort of fun activity and the three of them being together.

"Then we'll do Christmas Eve—it's open Christmas Eve day, right?" he asked her.

She smiled at Colin, happy to confirm at least this much for him. "Yes."

"Okay, then that's the plan," he finalized. "We'll go to Disneyland on Christmas Eve day and then figure out something different for Christmas Day." Ever positive, Colin tightened his arm around her shoulders, drawing her closer to him.

"How about celebrating it on the beach, just the three of us?" Ellie asked, the idea suddenly coming to her. "It's pretty down by Laguna Beach this time of year, and there're some trees and a few benches just a little ways in from the beach. There's even this picturesque gazebo overlooking the water," she recalled. "We could pack a lunch, eat there, then look for seashells or just walk along the sand." She shifted so she could look at him. "What do you think?"

"I think that I'm lucky to have you," Colin answered, hugging her to him. "Heather and I both are."

There it was again, that feeling that they were a

unit, a family. Ellie felt the same rosy glow she always did when she contemplated their situation.

A tiny voice in her head whispered, *It's not going to last. You know that. It's not going to last.*

Her sense of self-defense instantly kicked in, shutting down the voice and blocking it.

But even so, the little voice still insisted on echoing through her brain.

"C'mon, Jerry, get a move on. We've got two stories to cover and we're not going to cover them from here," Ellie urged.

It was several days after she and Colin had made their holidays plans and she had to admit, she was really looking forward to the day. She hadn't been to Disneyland as a visitor for *years*.

She'd already reached the doorway leading out of the newsroom bull pen and doubled back to her cameraman in the time it had taken Jerry to secure the camera case he always brought with him on assignments.

Jerry raised his eyes to look at her. "Looks like someone got a double dose of vitamins this morning," he commented. "Or are you just downing too many energy drinks?"

She laughed, dismissing his questions. "If you must know, I'm just being high on life," she informed the man.

Jerry gazed at her knowingly. "Is that what you call him these days? 'Life'?" he asked with a laugh, slinging the camera-case strap over his arm. It was heavy and required balance on his part, even given his height.

"I don't know what you're talking about," Ellie sniffed, pretending as if Jerry had no idea that her life had taken this turn for the better and why.

"Uh-huh. Sure. On to more important things," Jerry said, continuing. "Betsy and I are having our usual Christmas party this weekend. You're invited." He said it as if it was an afterthought instead of all part of the hazing that he loved putting her through. "Oh, and bring Mr. Life along," he added.

"We'll see," Ellie said, grabbing another one of Jerry's cases and automatically carrying it out for him. They were a team in her eyes and there was no hierarchy to their relationship. "You take more time getting ready than my grandmother," she said, shaking her head.

"Hey, I've met your grandmother. That's a really together lady," he told her.

Ellie just made a dismissive sound. Turning to walk out the door for a second time, she found that her way was unexpectedly blocked by the program manager.

The man didn't look happy.

"I'm glad I caught you," Marty said. Instead of his usual good-natured smile, the program manager had a rather grim expression on his face.

"What's up, Marty?" Ellie asked, silently telling herself not to start coming up with dire scenarios. She had to stop being paranoid. "You giving us a third story to cover?" She glanced at Jerry, but he had no idea why the program manager had come to them instead of the other way around, either. "We might not be able to get to it in time," she warned.

She got no further.

"Something just came down over the wire," Marty

told her. His voice had never sounded so serious, so bleak. Ellie immediately felt her stomach seizing up and then sinking.

"What is it, Marty?" she asked. "C'mon, you're scaring me. What just came in over the wire?"

"Fifteen minutes ago, a local detective foiled a robbery in progress. Two guys tried to pull off a home invasion."

"You said foiled," Ellie repeated, her voice seeming to echo in her head as she spoke. She was afraid to say anything more, waiting for Marty to fill her in. Praying he wasn't going to say something she couldn't bear to hear. But then why did he look this way?

"The two burglars were taken into custody before they could make off with anything."

He was doling out information.

Why?

Her breath suddenly backed up in her throat. She felt Jerry's hand on her shoulder, as if he was silently trying to help her brace herself. She didn't want to brace herself. She wanted this to be all right.

Ellie shrugged his hand away. Her eyes never leaving the program manager's face, she held her breath as she demanded, "And the local detective?"

"He's alive but in critical condition," Marty told her. "The ambulance took him to Bedford Presbyterian."

Her voice was shaking as she heard herself ask, "You have a name?"

Marty barely nodded before saying, "It's him, Ellie. It's Detective Benteen."

For just one turbulent moment, the immediate world shrank down to a pinprick. She thought she was going to pass out—just like the first time. It took everything she had merely to struggle back to consciousness. She wasn't going to faint! She was stronger than that.

But the next moment, Ellie just wanted to flee. To run and run until she was too exhausted to take another step. It didn't matter where, just away.

She couldn't go through this again, couldn't take the fear, the horrible pain waiting to rip her apart only a heartbeat away.

She'd been through this once; she couldn't go through this again.

She *couldn't.*

And then she heard Jerry's voice breaking through the fog about her brain.

"C'mon, I'll drive you," he told her, his hand up against her back as if he was afraid she'd sink to the floor if he took it away.

"I'm not covering this story," she all but snapped at him.

"I'm not driving you as a cameraman," he told her gently but firmly. "I'm driving you as a friend."

Stricken, Ellie realized she'd turned toward Marty and was looking at him questioningly.

The program manager waved her out. "Go—don't even think about it. I'll get someone else to cover your stories today."

Ellie didn't wait to hear anything more.

She didn't remember leaving the building, didn't remember the ride to the hospital. She was hardly aware of running through the hospital's electronic doors, which barely had time to open for her.

Jerry was the one who rattled off the information

to the woman sitting at the ER desk. Ellie just couldn't speak. Her legs and body were heavy. She felt as if she was walking through a nightmare.

A recurring nightmare.

She'd been in this hospital before, faced some woman at the ER desk before only to be told that her husband wasn't in any of the beds. Beds were for the living. He was in the morgue.

She was terrified of hearing that again. Terrified that it was happening all over again. That the person she had fallen in love with against every objection her common sense had raised had been ripped away from her by some madman firing a gun.

Just like last time.

Struggling to focus, to think, she only just realized that Jerry was talking to her.

"He's in surgery, Ellie. The nurse said Colin's in surgery."

Ellie stared up at the tall cameraman, her heart pounding so hard she could barely hear him. She blinked as if that could somehow clear her ears.

"Then he's alive?" she asked fearfully.

Jerry nodded, his curly reddish hair bobbing almost independently.

"He's alive," he confirmed, looking extremely relieved, then added, "They don't like to operate on dead people."

She tried to smile at the joke he'd made for her benefit, but she found that her mouth could hardly curve. Her face was frozen. Numb. The only thing she could do was repeat what Jerry had just told her. "He's alive."

And then, sobbing, she threw her arms around

Jerry, burying her face against the lower part of his chest because that was all she could reach.

Ellie pulled herself together long enough to call Olga to inform the woman of what had happened and to ask her to stay with Heather. She tried her very best to sound positive.

"He is going to be all right?" Olga asked, her tone demanding the information, the reassurance.

"He's going to be all right," Ellie told the woman, praying that if she said the words often enough, it would be so.

She terminated the call before her voice broke. She cried the second she stopped talking.

Ellie waited in the hall outside the operating door, leaning against the wall for support. Jerry stayed with her, refusing to leave her alone.

Someone brought out a couple of folding chairs for them. When Jerry opened the first one up, placing it beside Ellie, she dropped into it, her knees collapsing at that moment.

He opened the second one for himself.

"You don't have to stay with me," she told the cameraman as a second hour melted into a third.

"I'm not leaving you now, kid," he answered. "Besides, I'm your ride, remember?"

"I can call a cab," she told him numbly.

"Oh no," he told her. "You're not getting rid of me that easily." He shifted in the chair. It wasn't exactly comfortable for a big man like him. "You want something to drink?" he offered. "We might be here for a while. I think I saw a vending machine down the hall."

Ellie shook her head. "You go get something for yourself," she told him. "I'm okay."

She was far from okay, but he knew better than to argue with her. He merely noted, "Dehydrating yourself isn't going to do him any good." Rising, he told Ellie, "Be right back."

She was hardly aware of nodding. Her eyes remained trained on the operating room doors.

Jerry was just coming back when he saw the surgeon emerging from the operating room. The short, stocky older man didn't even need a moment to look around for her. Ellie was immediately on her feet, at his side.

As she confronted the doctor, her eyes begged him to give her something positive to hang on to.

"Are you here for Detective Benteen?" the surgeon asked.

"Yes!" And then Ellie's voice cracked a little. "Is he—"

She couldn't bring herself to continue. She was too afraid to ask the question. And even more afraid of the answer she might receive.

"He's out of surgery," the doctor told her just as Jerry reached her side. "It was touch and go for a while. Detective Benteen received one bullet to the thigh, one to the chest. The latter just barely missed a major artery. A little more to the left and he wouldn't have even made it to the hospital."

"How is he?" Jerry asked the doctor before Ellie was able to find her voice.

"He's stable now," the doctor told them in a monotone voice. It was obvious that he'd been through a great many of these life-and-death surgeries. "The next few hours will be critical. If he makes it through the night, there's every reason to believe that he'll make a full recovery." Only then did the doctor's tone begin to sound a little more optimistic. "There'll be some physical therapy involved and a lot of patience, but he should be good as new, given time."

Ellie's eyes were filled with tears and she had to blink several times just in order to see. Her throat felt completely parched and almost like leather as she cried, "Thank you, Doctor. Thank you!"

The surgeon merely nodded. "Detective Benteen's going to be in recovery for a while, and then he'll be taken to his room. I really doubt that he'll wake up before morning." He reconsidered his words. "Possibly even later than that. Why don't you go home and get some rest?" he suggested, looking from Ellie to the hulking figure beside her.

It was Jerry who told him, "Doc, she's not about to leave unless you get someone to carry her out. And he'd probably have to tie her up, as well."

"I understand," the surgeon replied. He had an alternate suggestion. "You might want to go to the cafeteria while you're waiting." With that, the doctor left.

"I'll bring you something to eat," Jerry volunteered. Tucking the can of diet soda he'd brought for her into her hands, Jerry put his own can on the folding chair and went to the cafeteria.

Chapter Seventeen

Colin's eyelids felt like lead.

He was certain that he'd opened his eyes a number of times, struggling each time, only to ultimately realize that he still hadn't even managed to pry his lids apart at all.

He needed to open his eyes, needed to see where he was and if everything was all right. There was a boy, a boy he was trying to save.

Colin kept struggling for what felt like an eternity and then, finally, *finally*, he managed to force open his eyelids.

It didn't help. He had no idea where he was.

Slowly, his brain began to make sense of the scene, processing the faint antiseptic smell mingling with the scent of vanilla and lavender.

A memory stirred, gradually taking shape.

That was her scent. Her perfume.

"Ellie?"

At the sound of his voice, Ellie jolted upright. She'd spent the better part of the last twenty hours in Colin's room, sitting in the world's most uncomfortable chair beside his bed. Somewhere along the line, she must have fallen asleep and now her body was loudly complaining about it. Complaining about the very awkward, pretzel-like position she'd wound up assuming.

She ached all over, but that sensation was a distant second to what she was experiencing right now: the most tremendous amount of relief she'd ever felt.

"Welcome back, Detective Benteen," she said, blinking back tears of joy. She dragged the chair a tiny bit closer; it was all the distance that remained between the bed and her.

"Where am I?" His ordinarily powerful voice came out in what sounded like a croak.

She allowed herself to touch his face, brushing the hair back out of his eyes. "Not in heaven," she informed him.

"You sure?" His voice faded for a moment. It took another moment before he could continue to speak. "Then why am I looking at an angel?"

Wanting to laugh and cry at the same time, Ellie took his hand in hers, grateful simply to be holding it, to feel the warmth of his flesh against hers. She touched it to her cheek.

He was alive!

"Oh, you're going to have to do better than that to make up for this," she informed him once she could find her voice again.

Details began to come back to him, choppy details

that were out of order. His brow furrowed as he tried to organize them to remember them the way they occurred. "I was shot."

Ellie nodded her head, still holding on to his hand tightly. "Good guess."

His eyes suddenly became alert as more details came rushing back, sharper now.

He remembered.

"What about the boy?" he asked her urgently. "Is the boy all right?"

Before he had finally and reluctantly left her, Jerry had called the station and gotten the full story that had come across the wire. There'd been a burglary in progress. Apparently, he'd told her, no one was supposed to be home. Nothing ever went according to plan. It turned out a twelve-year-old boy had been home from school, sick. It was the boy, hiding in his bedroom closet, who'd called 911 about the two thugs who were breaking in.

Because of his proximity when the call came in, Colin was the first on the scene. The burglars, two hardened criminals with two strikes against each of them, were armed. A gun battle ensued.

"The boy's fine. The studio's probably doing a story on his 911 call right now." She suppressed the urge to beat on Colin for rushing in alone like that. "Why didn't you wait for backup?" she asked.

Colin sank against his pillow, suddenly feeling very drained again. His eyelids were trying to close. "You know about that?"

"I know everything," she told him, her voice close to cracking again. "I'm a reporter, remember?"

His eyes were already drifting shut again. "Wanted

to get them…out of there…before…they found…the…
boy. Seemed…like a…good…idea at the…time."

He was asleep again.

Ellie sighed and settled back in the chair where
she'd been since he had been wheeled into the room
from recovery.

"I'll be here when you wake up," she quietly promised the detective.

The next time Colin woke up, he realized that Ellie
wasn't the only one in the room.

Seeing him open his eyes, his niece shrieked with
joy and threw her arms around his neck. Ellie didn't
have the heart to pull her away.

"You're alive!" Heather cried happily. "I was so
scared, so scared, Uncle Colin," she confessed, trying not to cry. "Ellie said not to worry, but I kinda
did, I did worry."

When he looked at Ellie over his niece's head, she
gave him the explanation she figured he was looking for. "Heather wanted to see for herself that you
were alive."

From the recess of the hospital room a third voice
joined in. "She would not believe me when I told her
you were going to be all right. She is stubborn, like
her uncle. So I brought her here because Ellie said
it would be all right," Olga informed him matter-of-
factly. "And now we will be going back," she said
in her no-nonsense tone, addressing Heather. "Your
uncle, he is needing to rest."

"Do as she says, kid," Colin told his niece fondly.
Smiling weakly, he stroked her hair. "I'll be home before you know it."

"You promise?" It wasn't a question; it was a plea for his solemn vow.

"I promise," he told her. "But Disneyland might have to wait for a while."

"I don't care about Disneyland," Heather told him with feeling, angry tears welling up in her eyes. "I just care about you."

Colin felt himself getting choked up. Trying to clear his throat, he looked at the woman who'd brought his niece in. "Thanks for bringing her, Olga."

"No need to be thanking me," she replied in her crisp manner. "Just remember to be ducking next time."

Putting her hands on the girl's shoulder, Olga began to herd Heather out of the room.

Belatedly, Ellie called after the girl, "I'll be by later."

Colin waited until Olga and his niece left before asking, "What's that about?"

"I'm just dropping off some of my things at your apartment later tonight," she told him.

Ellie had raised more questions for him than she'd answered. "Something going on I don't know about?" Colin asked.

"Lots of things going on that you don't know about," she told him mysteriously. And then, taking pity on the man, even if he was a damn fool who'd almost gotten himself killed, she said, "I'm moving in to take care of Heather while you're lying around here taking it easy. I don't want her life being disrupted any more than it already has."

"What about Olga?" he asked. For the last eight months, the woman had been his go-to babysitter.

"This is more than just watching her occasionally. Besides, Olga has a job. She can't afford to just take off for several weeks straight."

He supposed that made sense, but something else didn't.

"And you can?" he asked, remembering what she'd said about not being able to take a week off to go to Disney World.

"I put in for a leave of absence," she explained. Marty had told her to take as much time as she needed, assuring her that her job would be waiting for her when she got back. She smiled, grateful for the program manager's support. "Under the circumstances, I have a very understanding boss. So," she informed him, "like it or not, Detective Benteen, I am in this for the long haul."

It took effort because he was so tired, but Colin smiled. "Oh, I like it," he told her. "I like it very much."

Ellie made no response. She didn't want him thinking that she was trying to play what had happened— and his temporary disability—to her advantage. All she wanted was for him to get well.

She cleared her throat, then said, "Now, if you're through playing twenty questions, you have a menu to fill out. You're going to be here for at least a few days, so you might as well have them bring you something you like to eat."

Colin waved his hand dismissively—or tried to. He just didn't have the energy for it.

"Pick anything," he told her, a wave of exhaustion washing over him. "I'm easy."

Stunned, Ellie raised her eyes to look at him. "Not

hardly." And then she looked closer. "And…he's asleep again," she murmured to herself.

Resigned, she sat down with the hospital's menus and began to fill out the selections for only the next three days, fervently hoping that she wasn't being overly optimistic.

"You're not ready to go back to work," Ellie protested loudly as she watched Colin getting dressed in his bedroom.

For the last six weeks, for Heather's sake, she'd spent her nights on his living room couch. She'd cooked their meals and overseen every one of his physical therapy exercises. All along she'd watched Colin get progressively better with what seemed like a vengeance.

Very gently, he put his hands on her shoulders and moved Ellie out of his way. He took his shirt from the closet and began to put it on.

"The doctor just gave me a clean bill of health and cleared me for duty," he informed her.

Like she cared what the doctor said. Ellie made a dismissive noise, telling him what she thought of the doctor and his clearance.

"Well, I'm not ready to clear you for duty," she stated.

"Ellie, I can't go on just hiding in my apartment," he pointed out. Finished buttoning his shirt, he tucked it into his pants.

"Why not?" she asked. "At least it's safe here. Nobody's going to shoot you in your apartment," Ellie pointed out.

Colin stated the obvious, thinking of the incident

that had taken him out of commission these last six weeks. "Unless they break in."

"Pancakes would never let them—as long as you don't lock her up in that puppy crate," she specified. "Maybe you haven't noticed, but she's been your shadow the entire time you've been home." There had been a change in the dog since Colin had come home from the hospital. "It's like she can sense you've been hurt and she wants to protect you."

"If she does, it's because she's taking her cues from you." Done getting dressed, Colin took her into his arms. "Not that it hasn't been great being with you, having you bully me around," he deadpanned, referring to the physical therapy session he'd endured in order to be able to walk without a limp, "but you need to get back to work and so do I."

"What if you get shot again?" she challenged. She managed to keep the fear out of her voice, but there was no way she could keep it out of her heart.

He wasn't about to tell her he was bulletproof. "I can't tell you that I won't—"

"Terrific," Ellie bit off.

He had to go in, but he didn't want to leave her like this. He wanted her to understand. "Life doesn't come with guarantees, Ellie—you know that. You could get killed covering your next story," he pointed out.

She frowned, shaking her head. "I do mainly fluff pieces."

"Mainly, but not always. For that matter," he stressed, "a gas main could blow up just as you're going to your next location."

Okay, now he was really reaching, she thought. "That's not exactly a regular occurrence."

"Neither is my getting shot." He took her hands in his. "Honey, the important thing is that we make the very most of every minute we have."

"I just want to have more minutes," she told him, even as she knew that she couldn't stand in his way. It made her feel completely helpless.

Colin grinned. "I'm glad you said that."

"You are?"

"Yes—" he released one of her hands and put his into his jacket pocket, reaching in for something "—because then you make this easier for me to ask."

Ellie thought she knew where this was going. "You're talking about Disney World again, aren't you?" she asked. "Because I don't think—"

"No," Colin said, cutting her off. "I'm talking about this."

"This" turned out to be the black velvet box that he was holding in the palm of his hand. He held it up to her, expecting her to take it.

Ellie stared at the box and then at him, but she made no move to take it from him.

"What is it?" she whispered.

Since she wasn't taking the box from him or even opening it, he opened it for her.

Inside the box was a gleaming marquise-shaped diamond engagement ring.

When had he had time to buy this? She looked at him with confusion. "I've been with you the entire time you've been home from the hospital. How did you—?"

"I bought this before I got shot. I was going to ask you to marry me at Christmas," he explained.

"Then why didn't you?" Ellie asked. It didn't make sense to her.

"Because I got shot," he repeated, "and I didn't want to propose to you while you were here taking care of Heather and me. I didn't want you saying yes to my proposal because you felt sorry for me."

"So you're asking me while I'm angry at you?"

This was getting too involved. He wanted to keep it simple. "I was hoping that this would make you less angry." He slipped it on her finger while he made his argument. "I love you, Ellie. I can promise to love you for as long as I live—and then do my damnedest to live for a very long time."

She still wasn't saying anything.

Colin took a deep breath and made his final offer, "If you want me to stop being a cop—"

"Yes, yes, I do," she cried. "With all my heart, I do. But you are a cop—it's what you do, who you are, and I have no right to ask you to change, because I don't want you to change. I wouldn't want you to want me to change, so I have no right to dictate any conditions," she explained. Ellie slipped her arms around his neck. "I fell in love with a cop, heaven help me, and I guess I'm going to stay in love with a cop."

He encircled her waist, holding her close to him. "So, is that a yes?"

She smiled up into his eyes. "You're a clever cop. You figure it out," she challenged.

Colin drew her closer still. For the last six weeks, he had remained celibate. He'd been too weak in the beginning and then it seemed as if either Heather or Olga or both were always around, not to mention that there'd been an endless stream of visitors and well-wishers who kept dropping by. It was never just the two of them.

It was now. Olga had taken Heather to school a little while ago.

"You know," Colin told her, "I can be late on my first day getting back."

She could feel him wanting her. "What is it that you have in mind?"

He pressed a kiss to the side of her neck before answering. "Making love with my fiancée."

She could feel herself melting already. "So you're assuming that I'm saying yes?"

"Not assuming," Colin corrected. "Praying."

Ellie smiled then, a warm smile that began in her eyes and radiated all through her, pulling him in.

"Well, lucky for you, sometimes prayers *are* answered." And then, in case there was any lingering doubt, she said, "Just to make it official, yes, Detective Benteen, I will marry you. Since you stole my heart, you might as well have the rest of me."

Colin had nothing to say about that. He couldn't. He was far too busy kissing her and making good on what he'd just promised to do.

Epilogue

Cecilia had been watching for her.

The moment she spotted Olga entering the church, she half stood up in the pew and waved the woman over.

"Olga, come sit by us," Cilia called to her in what amounted to a stage whisper.

Olga approached the pew hesitantly, recognizing her employer as well as the woman's friends Theresa Manetti and Maizie Sommers, women she'd had the occasion to meet several times in passing.

"It is all right?" Olga asked, not wanting to intrude.

"More than all right," Maizie assured the woman with a welcoming laugh. She scooted over, as did Theresa and Cilia, as well as a woman Olga didn't know, creating room for the newcomer. "If it weren't for you, this might not be taking place."

Once Olga was seated, the fourth woman rose to her feet.

"I'd better take my place up front," Ellie's mother told the others. "I don't know how to thank you," Connie Williams said, repeating the sentiment she'd voiced earlier as her eyes swept over the four women. "I've never seen Ellie looking happier. Anything you want," she told them, "*anything*, I'm in your debt."

"Our pleasure," Maizie told her friend. "It's what we all really enjoy doing, isn't it, ladies?" She addressed her question to her friends.

But it was Olga who spoke up as soon as Ellie's mother had eased herself out of the pew and made her way up to the front of the church.

"This is what they call matchmaking, yes?" the woman asked, looking from Cilia to the other two.

Cilia's smile answered her, but just in case Olga needed more verification, Theresa told her, "Yes."

Olga nodded, a satisfied, somewhat thoughtful expression on her face.

"I think I like this matchmaking. Can we be doing this again?" She looked from one woman to the other, waiting for an answer.

"You bet your buttons we will," Maizie said with a laugh, her eyes glinting with amusement as well as pleasure.

"We will be needing buttons?" Olga asked, confused as she slanted a glance in Cilia's direction.

Cilia placed a hand on the other woman's wrist. "No, dear, no buttons."

Olga's brow furrowed. Not for the first time she thought that English was a very confusing language to learn. "But—"

"You'll get used to Maizie," Cilia promised.

"Shh, it's starting," Theresa said as the strains of the wedding march began to slowly swell and fill the packed church.

Everyone rose in anticipation.

Wordlessly, her eyes fixed to the rear doors, waiting for them to part, Maizie automatically passed out three tissues she'd brought with her in her clutch purse, one for each of the women in the pew. She kept a fourth one for herself. Weddings never failed to make them tear up. She saw no reason to think that this wedding would be different.

Especially not when she saw Heather entering first, positively glowing as she took measured steps into the church, a flower basket in her hand.

Grabbing small fistfuls of rose petals in her hand, Heather happily paved the path before her with a mixture of pink and white.

And then Ellie entered, resplendent in a floor-length wedding dress, a wreath of flowers in her hair and clutching a cascading arrangement of pink and white roses in her hands.

"They just keep getting more lovely, don't they?" Theresa whispered to her friends.

"She's breathtaking," Cilia agreed.

"Colin certainly seems to think so," Maizie observed, directing their attention toward the groom.

"And that, in the end, is all that matters," Olga said in finality, adding her voice to theirs.

All three old friends exchanged looks and smiled just as Ellie reached the front of the altar, ready to join her life with the man who stood there waiting for her.

Attuned to one another's thoughts, they had no need to voice what they were all thinking: another undertaking well done.

* * * * *

Don't miss Marie Ferrarella's next
Harlequin Special Edition,
FORTUNE'S SECOND CHANCE COWBOY
the third book in
THE FORTUNES OF TEXAS:
THE SECRET FORTUNES
continuity, available March 2017!

*Can't get enough romance? Keep reading for
a special preview of WILD HORSE SPRINGS,
the latest engrossing novel in
the* RANSOM CANYON *series
by* New York Times *bestselling author
Jodi Thomas,
coming in February 2017 from HQN Books!*

CODY WINSLOW THUNDERED through the night on a half-wild horse that loved to run. The moon followed them, dancing along the edge of the canyon as they darted over winter buffalo grass that was stiff with frost.

The former Texas Ranger watched the dark outline of the earth where the land cracked open wide enough for a river to run at its base.

The canyon's edge seemed to snake closer, as if it were moving, crawling over the flat plains, daring Cody to challenge death. One missed step might take him and the horse over the rim and into the black hole. They'd tumble maybe a hundred feet down, barreling over jagged rocks and frozen juniper branches as sharp as spears. No horse or man would survive.

Only, tonight Cody wasn't worried. He needed to ride, to run, to feel adrenaline pumping in his veins, to know he was alive. He rode hoping to outrun his dark mood. The demons that were always in his mind were chasing him tonight. Daring him. Betting him to take one more risk…the one that would finally kill him.

"Run," he shouted to the midnight mare. Nothing would catch him here. Not on his land. Not over land his ancestors had hunted on for thousands of years. Fought over. Died for and bled into. Apache blood, settler blood, Comanchero blood mixed in him as it did in this part of Texas. His family tree was a tumbleweed of every kind of tribe that ever crossed the plains.

If the horse fell and they went to their deaths, no one would find them for weeks on this far corner of his ranch. Even the canyon that snaked off the great Palo Duro had no name here. It wasn't beautiful like Ransom Canyon, with layers of earth revealed in a rainbow of colors. Here the rocks were jagged, shooting out of the deep earthen walls from twenty feet in some places, almost like a thin shelf.

The petrified-wood formations along the floor of the canyon reminded Cody of snipers waiting, unseen but deadly. Cody felt numb, already dead inside, as he raced across a place with no name on a horse he called Midnight.

The horse's hooves tapped suddenly over a low place where water ran off the flat land and into the canyon. Frozen now. Silent. Deadly black ice. For a moment the tapping matched Cody's heartbeat, then both horse and rider seemed to realize the danger at once.

Cody leaned back, pulling the reins, hoping to stop the animal in time, but the horse reared in panic. Dancing on her hind legs for a moment before twisting violently and bucking Cody off.

As Cody flew through the night air, he almost smiled. The battle he'd been fighting since he was shot and left for dead on the border three years ago was about to end here on his own land. The voices of all the ancestors who came before him whispered in the wind, as if calling him.

When he hit the frozen ground so hard it knocked the air from his lungs, he knew death wouldn't come easy tonight. Though he'd welcome the silence, Cody knew he'd fight to the end. He came from generations of fighters. He was the last of his line, and here in the dark he'd make his stand. Too far away to call for help. And too stubborn to ask anyway.

As he fought to breathe, his body slid over a tiny river of frozen rain and into the black canyon.

He twisted, struggling to stop, but all he managed to do was tumble down. Branches whipped against him, and rocks punched his ribs with the force of a prizefighter's blow. And still he rolled. Over and over. Ice on his skin, warm blood dripping into his eyes. He tried bracing for the hits that came when he landed for a moment before his body rolled again. He grabbed for a rock or a branch to hold on to, but his leather gloves couldn't get a grip on the ice.

He wasn't sure if he managed to relax or pass out, but when he landed on a flat rock near the bottom of the canyon, total blackness surrounded him and the few stars above offered no light. For a while he lay still, aware that he was breathing. A good sign. He hurt all over. More proof he was alive.

He'd been near death before. He knew that sometimes the body turned off the pain. Slowly, he mentally took inventory. There were parts that hurt like hell. Others he couldn't feel at all.

Cody swore as loud as he could and smiled. At least he had his voice. Not that anyone would hear him in the canyon. Maybe his brain was mush; he obviously had a head wound. The blood kept dripping into his eyes. His left leg throbbed with each heartbeat and he couldn't draw a deep breath. He swore again.

He tried to move and pain skyrocketed, forcing him

to concentrate to stop shaking. Fire shot up his leg and flowed straight to his heart. Cody took shallow breaths and tried to reason. He had to control his breathing. He had to stay awake or he'd freeze. He had to keep fighting. Survival was bone and blood to his nature.

The memory of his night in the mud near the Rio Grande came back as if it had been only a day ago, not three years. He'd been bleeding then, hurt, alone. Four rangers had stood on the bank at dusk. He'd seen the other three crumple when bullets fell like rain.

Only, it had been hot that night, so silent after all the gunfire. Cody had known that every ranger in the area would be looking for him at first light; he had to make it to dawn first. Stay alive. They'd find him.

But not this time.

No one would look for him tonight or tomorrow. No one would even notice he was gone. He'd made sure of that. He'd left all his friends back in Austin after the shooting. He'd broken up with his girlfriend, who'd said she couldn't deal with hospitals. When he came back to his family's land, he didn't bother to call any of his old friends. He'd grown accustomed to the solitude. He'd needed it to heal not just the wounds outside, but the ones deep inside.

Cody swore again.

The pain won out for a moment and his mind drifted. At the corners of his consciousness, he knew he needed to move, stop the bleeding, try not to freeze, but he'd become an expert at drifting that night on the border. Even when a rifle had poked into his chest as one of the drug runners tested to see if he was alive, Cody hadn't reacted.

If he had, another bullet would have gone into his body, which was already riddled with lead.

Cody recited the words he'd once had to scrub off the walls in grade school. Mrs. Presley had kept repeating as he worked, *Cody Winslow, you'll die cussing if you don't learn better.*

Turned out she might be right. Even with his eyes almost closed, the stars grew brighter and circled around him like drunken fireflies. If this was death's door, he planned to go through yelling.

The stars drew closer. Their light bounced off the black canyon walls as if they were sparks of echoes.

He stopped swearing as the lights began to talk.

"He's dead," one high, bossy voice said. "Look how shiny the blood is."

Tiny beams of light found his face, blinding him to all else.

A squeaky sound added, "I'm going to throw up. I can't look at blood."

"No, he's not dead," another argued. "His hand is twitching and if you throw up, Marjorie Martin, I'll tell Miss Adams."

All at once the lights were bouncing around him, high voices talking over each other.

"Yes, he is dead."

"Stop saying that."

"You stop saying anything."

"I'm going to throw up."

Cody opened his eyes. The lights were circling around him like a war party.

"See, I told you so."

One beam of light came closer, blinding him for a moment, and he blinked.

"He's hurt. I can see blood bubbling out of him in several spots." The bossy voice added, "Don't touch it, Marjorie. People bleeding have germs."

The gang of lights streamed along his body as if trying to torture him or drive him mad as the world kept changing from black to bright. It occurred to him that maybe he was being abducted by aliens, but he doubted the beings coming to conquer the world would land here in West Texas or that they'd sound like little girls.

"Hell," he said and to his surprise the shadows all jumped back.

After a few seconds he made out the outline of what might be a little girl, or maybe ET.

"You shouldn't cuss, mister. We heard you way back in the canyon yelling out words I've seen written but never knew how to pronounce."

"Glad I could help with your education, kid. Any chance you have a cell phone or a leader?"

"We're not allowed to carry cell phones. It interferes with our communicating with nature." She shone her flashlight in his eyes. "Don't call me *kid.* Miss Adams says you should address people by their names. It's more polite. My name is Melanie Miller and I could read before I started kindergarten."

Cody mumbled a few words, deciding he was in hell already and, who knew, all the helpers' names started with *M.*

All at once the lights went jittery again and every one of the six little girls seemed to be talking at the same time.

One thought he was too bloody to live. One suggested they should cover him with their coats; another voted for undressing him. Two said they would never touch blood. One wanted to put a tourniquet around his neck.

Cody was starting to hope death might come faster when another shadow carrying a lantern moved into the mix. "Move back, girls. This man is hurt."

He couldn't see more than an outline, but the new arrival was definitely not a little girl. Tall, nicely shaped, hiking boots, a backpack on her back.

Closing his eyes and ignoring the little girls' constant questions, he listened as a calm voice used her cell to call for help. She had the location down to latitude and longitude and described a van parked in an open field about a hundred yards from her location where they could land a helicopter. When she hung up, she knelt at his side and shifted the backpack off her shoulder.

As she began to check his injuries, her voice calmly gave instructions. "Go back to the van, girls. Two at a time, take turns flashing your lights at the sky toward the North Star. The rest of you get under the blankets and stay warm. When you hear the chopper arrive, you can watch from the windows, but stay in the van.

"McKenna, you're in charge. I'll be back as soon as they come."

Another *M*, Cody thought, but didn't bother to ask.

To his surprise the gang of ponytails marched off like tiny little soldiers.

"How'd you find me?" Cody asked the first of a dozen questions bouncing around in his aching head as the woman laid out supplies from her pack.

"Your cussing echoed off the canyon wall for twenty miles." Her hands moved along his body, not in a caress, but to a man who hadn't felt a woman's touch in years, it wasn't far from it.

"Want to give me your name? Know what day it is? What year? Where you are?"

"I don't have brain damage," he snapped, then regretted moving his head. "My name's Winslow. I don't care what day it is or what year for that matter." He couldn't make out her face. "I'm on my own land. Or at least I was when my horse threw me."

She might have been pretty if she wasn't glaring at him. The lantern light offered that flashlight-to-the-chin kind of glow.

"Where does it hurt?" She kept her voice low, but she didn't sound friendly. "As soon as I pass you to the medics, I'll start looking for your horse. The animal might be out here, too, hurting or dead. Did he fall with you?"

Great! His Good Samaritan was worried more about the horse than him. "I don't know. I don't think so. When I fell off the edge of the canyon, Midnight was still standing, probably laughing at me." He took a breath as the woman moved to his legs. "I tumbled for what seemed like miles. It hurts all over."

"How did this happen?"

"The horse got spooked when we hit a patch of ice," he snapped again, tired of talking, needing all his strength to handle the pain. Cusswords flowed out with each breath. Not at her, but at his bad luck.

She ignored them as she brushed over the left leg of his jeans already stained dark with blood. He tried to keep from screaming. He fought her hand as she searched, examining, and he knew he couldn't take much more without passing out.

"Easy," she whispered as her blood-warmed fingers cupped his face. "Easy, cowboy. You've got a bad break. I have to do what I can to stabilize you and slow the blood flow. They'll be here soon. You've got to let me wrap a few of these wounds so you don't bleed out."

He nodded once, knowing she was right.

In the glow of a lantern she worked, making a tourniquet out of his belt, carefully wrapping his leg, then his head wound.

Her voice finally came low, sexy maybe if it were a different time, a different place. "It looks bad, but I don't see any chunks of brain poking out anywhere."

He didn't know if she was trying to be funny or just stating a fact. He didn't bother to laugh. She put a bandage on the gash along his throat. It wasn't deep, but it dripped a steady stream of blood.

As she wrapped the bandage, her breasts brushed against his cheek, distracting him. If this was her idea of doctoring a patient with no painkillers, it was working. For a few seconds there, he almost forgot to hurt.

"I don't have water to clean the wounds, but the dressing should keep anything else from getting in."

Cody began to calm. The pain was still there, but the demons in the corners of his mind were silent. Watching her move in the shadows relaxed him.

"Cody," he finally said. "My first name is Cody."

She smiled then for just a second.

"You a nurse?" he asked.

"No. I'm a park ranger. If you've no objection, I'd like to examine your chest next."

Cody didn't move as she unzipped his jacket. "I used to be a ranger, but I never stepped foot in a park."

He could feel her unbuttoning his shirt. Her hand moved in, gently gliding across his ribs.

When he gasped for air, she hesitated, then whispered, "One broken rib." A moment later she added, "Two."

He forced slow, long breaths as he felt the cold night air pressing against his bare chest. Her hand crossed over his bruised skin, stopping at the scars he'd collected that night at the Rio Grande.

She lifted the light. "Bullet wounds?" she questioned more to herself than him. "You've been hurt bad before."

"Yeah," he said as he took back control of his mind and made light of a gunfight that almost ended his life. "I was fighting outlaws along the Rio Grande. I swear it seemed like that night almost two hundred years ago. Back when Captain Hays ordered his men to cross the river with guns blazing. We went across just like that, only chasing drug runners and not cattle rustlers like they did back then. But we were breaking the law not to cross just the same."

He closed his eyes and saw his three friends. They'd gone through training together and were as close as brothers. They wanted to fight for right. They thought they were invincible that night on the border, just like Captain Hays's men must have believed.

Only, those rangers had won the battle. They'd all returned to Texas. Cody had carried his best friend back across the water that night three years ago, but Hobbs hadn't made it. He'd died in the mud a few feet from Cody. Fletcher took two bullets but helped Gomez back across. Both men died.

"I've heard of that story about the famous Captain

Hays." She brought him back from a battle that had haunted him every night for three years. "Legend is that not one ranger died that night. They rode across the Rio screaming and firing. The bandits thought there were a hundred of them coming. But, cowboy, if you rode with Hays, that'd make you a ghost tonight and you feel like flesh and blood to me. Today's rangers are not allowed to cross."

Her hand was moving over his chest lightly, caressing now, calming him, letting him know that she was near. He relaxed and wished they were somewhere warm.

"You're going to make it, Winslow. I have a feeling you're too tough to die easy."

Don't miss WILD HORSE SPRINGS by
New York Times *bestselling author Jodi Thomas,*
available February 2017 wherever
HQN books and ebooks are sold!

www.Harlequin.com

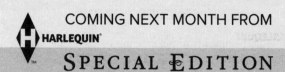

Wrapped more tightly in the shawl, she clomped across the wooden porch, the sound then muffled in the dirt as she made her way past the paddock to the foreman's cabin. The clear, starry night was silent and still, save for the thrum of crickets' chirping, the distant howl of a coyote. The cabin's front door swung open before she reached Colin's porch, a spear of light guiding her way. And with that, the full ramifications of what she was doing—or about to do, anyway—slammed into her.

But she had no idea what it might mean to Colin, she thought as his broad-shouldered silhouette filled the doorway, fragmenting the light. Maybe nothing, really— oh, hell, her heart was about to pound right out of her chest—since men were much more adept at these things than women. Weren't they?

Spudsy scampered out onto the porch from behind Colin's feet, wriggling up a storm when he saw her, and Emily's heart stopped its whomping long enough to squeeze at the sight of the bundle of furry joy she'd come to love.

At least she'd be able to keep the dog, she thought as she scooped up the little puppy to bury her face in his ruff, trying to ignore Colin's piercing gaze.

Oh, hell. That whole "sex as fun" thing? Who was she kidding? That wasn't her. Never had been. What on earth had made her think a single event would change *her*?

Although this one just might.

"I made a fire," Colin said quietly. Carefully. As though afraid she might spook. Never mind this had been her idea.

"That's nice."

Ergh.

Something like a smile ghosted around his mouth. "We can always just talk. No expectations. Isn't that what you said?" He shoved his hands into his pockets. "You're safe, honey. With me." His lips curved. "*From* me."

Still cuddling the puppy, she came up onto the porch. Closer. Too close. But not so close that she couldn't, if she were so inclined, still grab common sense by the hand and run like hell.

"And from myself?"

"That, I can't help you with."

Another step closer. Then another, each one a little farther away from common sense, whimpering in the dust behind her. "Kiss me," she whispered.

Don't miss
FALLING FOR THE REBOUND BRIDE
by Karen Templeton,
available February 2017 wherever
Harlequin® Special Edition books and ebooks are sold.

www.Harlequin.com

Turn your love of reading into rewards you'll love with
Harlequin My Rewards

**Join for FREE today at
www.HarlequinMyRewards.com**

Earn **FREE BOOKS** of your choice.

Experience **EXCLUSIVE OFFERS** and contests.

Enjoy **BOOK RECOMMENDATIONS**
selected just for you.

PLUS! Sign up now
and get **500** points
right away!

Earn **FREE REWARDS**
Join Today!
HarlequinMyRewards.com

MYR16R

HARLEQUIN®

A *Romance* FOR EVERY MOOD™

JUST CAN'T GET ENOUGH?

Join our social communities
and talk to us online.

You will have access to the latest
news on upcoming titles and special
promotions, but most importantly,
you can talk to other fans about your
favorite Harlequin reads.

Harlequin.com/Community

Facebook.com/HarlequinBooks

Twitter.com/HarlequinBooks

Pinterest.com/HarlequinBooks

HSOCIAL

THE WORLD IS BETTER WITH

Romance

Harlequin® has everything from contemporary, passionate and heartwarming to suspenseful and inspirational stories.

Whatever your mood, we have a romance just for you!

Connect with us to find your next great read, special offers and more.

 /HarlequinBooks

 @HarlequinBooks

www.HarlequinBlog.com

www.Harlequin.com/Newsletters

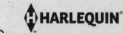

HARLEQUIN®

A *Romance* FOR EVERY MOOD™

www.Harlequin.com

SERIESHALOAD2015